Girl Politics

Nancy Rue

Other books in the growing Faithgirlz!™ library

The Faithgirlz!™ Bible
NIV Faithgirlz!™ Backpack Bible
My Faithgirlz!™ Journal

The Sophie Series

Sophie's World (Book One)
Sophie's Secret (Book Two)
Sophie Under Pressure (Book Three)
Sophie Steps Up (Book Four)
Sophie's First Dance (Book Five)
Sophie's Stormy Summer (Book Six)
Sophie's Friendship Fiasco (Book Seven)
Sophie and the New Girl (Book Eight)
Sophie Flakes Out (Book Nine)
Sophie Loves Jimmy (Book Ten)
Sophie's Drama (Book Eleven)
Sophie Gets Real (Book Twelve)

Nonfiction

Everybody Tells Me to Be Myself but I Don't Know Who I Am
The Skin You're In: Discovering True Beauty
Body Talk
No Boys Allowed: Devotions for Girls
Girlz Rock: Devotions for Girls
Chick Chat: Devotions for Girls
Shine On, Girl!: Devotions for Girls

Check out www.faithgirlz.com

faiThGirLz!

Girl Politics

Friends,
Cliques,
and
Really Mean
Chicks

Nancy Rue

 ZONDERkidz

ZONDERVAN.com/
AUTHORTRACKER
follow your favorite authors

So we fix our eyes not on what is seen, but on what
is unseen. For what is seen is temporary, but what is
unseen is eternal.

—2 Corinthians 4:18

ZONDERKIDZ

Girl Politics
Copyright © 2007 by Nancy Rue

Requests for information should be addressed to:

Zonderkidz, *Grand Rapids, Michigan* 49530

Library of Congress Cataloging-in-Publication Data

Rue, Nancy N.
    Girl politics : friends, cliques, and really mean chicks / by Nancy Rue.
       p.   cm—(Faithgirlz)
     ISBN 978-0-310-71296-1 (softcover)
     1. Female friendship—Juvenile literature. 2. Friendship—Juvenile literature. 3. Bullying in
schools—Juvenile literature. 4. Christian life—Juvenile literature. I. Title.
BF575.F66R84 2007
241'.676208342—dc22   2007022891

All Scripture quotations, unless otherwise indicated, are taken from the Holy Bible, *New International
Version®*, *NIV®*. Copyright © 1973, 1978, 1984 by Biblica, Inc.™ Used by permission of Zondervan. All
rights reserved worldwide.

Any Internet addresses (websites, blogs, etc.) and telephone numbers printed in this book are offered
as a resource. They are not intended in any way to be or imply an endorsement by Zondervan, nor does
Zondervan vouch for the content of these sites and numbers for the life of this book.

Scripture quotations marked "The Message" are taken from *The Message*. Copyright © by Eugene H.
Peterson 1993, 1994, 1995, 1996, 2000, 2001, 2002. Used by permission of NavPress Publishing Group.

Published in association with the literary agency of Alive Communications, Inc., 7680 Goddard Street,
Suite 200, Colorado Springs, CO 80920. www.alivecommunications.com

Zonderkidz is a trademark of Zondervan.

Editor: Barbara Scott
Interior design: Sherri L. Hoffman
Art direction and cover design: Merit Kathan

Printed in the United States of America

11 12 13 14 15 16 17 18 19 20 /DCI/ 23 22 21 20 19 18 17 16 15 14 13 12 11 10 9 8

Contents

chapter one

What's a Girl Thing ...
AND WHAT'S NOT?

E mily Ellen Edwards was having a very strange day.

It started to get weird when she slipped into her usual seat on the school bus. Her best friend Lara Lillo was there, of course. But this morning she barely gave Emily a glance before she zipped her eyes back to someone in the seat in front of them.

It was Katy Cuthbert — the girl who practically kept the price tags on her clothes so everyone would know how expensive they were. She even had her nails done — in the fifth grade — hello-o! Emily and Lara and the rest of their friends didn't talk to her that much because *obviously* Katy thought she was way better than they were.

But there she was, hands cupped around Lara's ear, whispering into it. *Whispering.* Like a best friend.

When Katy turned to another Price Tag Girl who slipped in beside her at the next stop, Emily caught Lara by the sleeve and hissed into her other ear.

"What's going on?"

"Huh?"

"What was Katy Cutthroat talking to you about?"

"Nothing," Lara said.

Emily lowered her chin. "Hello-o! She was flapping her lips, like, nine hundred miles an hour. She must have been saying *something*."

Lara rolled her eyes. "Something about herself — *of course*."

Okay. That was better.

When they got to school and everyone was in their seats, Emily wrote Lara a note.

I'm glad you're my best friend.

Lara wrote back, *Totally.*

Then why, when it was time to pick their groups for the social studies project, did Lara let Katy drag her into the circle she'd made with the other girls who had French manicures?

"Come on, Em," Lara said over her shoulder.

Emily followed, feeling like a pitiful puppy.

Katy patted the chair beside her for Lara to sit in. That left no place for Emily. Katy gave Emily a smile like the plastic lips on Mr. Potato Head.

"Looks like you'll have to find a different group," Katy said.

"I could pull up another chair," Emily said.

"We have enough people," Katy said.

Emily looked quickly at Lara, but she was staring down at her cuticles. Her cheeks were the color of cranberries.

"La-ra," Emily said between tightened teeth.

"Sorry," Lara said. She didn't even look up.

Emily stumbled over to her two almost-best friends, who had obviously witnessed the entire scene. They pulled a chair in close to theirs and tugged Emily into it. Kimberly's eyes were blazing. Mary Elizabeth's were shooting glares at Lara like little gun barrels.

"I can't believe Lara did that to you!" Kimberly said in a whisper.

"To *us*," Mary Elizabeth said, *not* in a whisper.

Kimberly leaned toward Emily. "Don't even worry about it, Em. We'll have our own group."

"And not just for this project." Mary Elizabeth shot a few more eye bullets at Lara. "For real. Like, all the time."

"Just wait 'til she tries to sit with us at lunch," Kimberly said. "Then she'll see how it feels."

Mary Elizabeth nodded. "That's what she gets for ditching us. Right, Em?"

"Sure," Emily said in a tiny voice. But she wanted to shout, *Lara! What just happened? We're best friends!*

Her mind spun. This was really strange. It was absolutely weird.

And it hurt like nothing else.

now what?

If you are a girl between the ages of eight and twelve, you have probably faced something like what Emily is going through. Or maybe your situation has been more like Lara's, or Kimberly and Mary Elizabeth's, or even Katy's. If none of those kinds of things have happened to you, they just might. That's because you're still learning about friendship, which, though fun, can get pretty complicated. This book is here to help you

* know what real friendship is like,
* fix the mistakes everyone makes from time to time in relationships,
* avoid the major bummers like cliques and bullying, and
* help make your girl community a safe place for every girl to be her true self.

Let's get back to poor Emily. What do you think she should do about Lara, about Mary Elizabeth and Kimberly, and about Katy and the Price Tag Girls? Decide what you would say to her if you were there with her and write it in the space below. There are no right or wrong answers, so be honest. If, as you read the rest of this book, you discover something that makes you change your mind about how to encourage Emily, you'll have a chance to "talk" to her again in the last chapter.

Dear Emily…

Here's the Deal

Can you imagine what it would be like not to have at least one girlfriend? Think about it. What would you do

* at lunchtime?
* at recess?
* when something freaky happened to you?
* when something cool happened to you?
* when you were bored?
* when your feelings were hurt?

Even worse, how would you *feel*? (Hopefully you don't feel that way right now, but if you do, this book can really help. Read with hope.)

Circle any of these words that describe what it would be like to be girlfriend-less. Add your own if you think of some.

Sad   Scared

Lonely   Anxious

Freaked-out   Angry   Depressed

Lost   Hurt   Confused

Bored

It would definitely be a drag, huh? Having friends is probably one of the things that makes you happiest. That's because you're getting to be more independent, which prepares you for becoming a grown-up. Although your family is probably the center of your life, becoming attached to girls your own age means you're learning that you can — and should — have relationships with people other than Mom, Dad, brothers, sisters, and anybody else who's related to you. They all just naturally love you because you're part of them (even if your brothers and sisters don't always show it!). When you make friends, people love you who don't have to!

Having friends is how you figure out

* how to get along with people;
* what kind of people you want to hang out with;
* what you're like when there's conflict (you know, like dis-agreements, arguments, fights); and
* how important friendship is — because you'll need and want it all your life.

Besides all that, having friends is the best, especially that one BFF (Best Friend Forever) so you can

* giggle together until you can't breathe;
* have a whole conversation from opposite sides of the room without saying a word;
* finish each other's sentences;
* speak your own special language;
* tell her things you wouldn't share with anybody else;
* stand up for each other when the world is mean; and
* be absolutely yourself when you're together.

Perfect, huh? Well, not always. Certain stuff happens in every friendship and in every girl-group relationship — stuff that takes some work:

* A girl is accidentally left out now and then.
* An old friend drifts away.
* There are occasional arguments and splits and getting back together.
* Feelings get hurt without anybody meaning for it to happen — like name-calling for fun.
* Jealousies arise once in a while.
* You get annoyed with each other on occasion (imagine that!).
* A girl doesn't fit into one group for some reason so she finds another one.
* You realize a friendship is bad for you, and you have to break it off.

That's all normal stuff. It's *hard* normal stuff, but it offers you a chance to learn how to work things out with people. This book is here to help you fix the problems and keep them from happening so often. If you use what you learn here, your friendships will turn into a sisterhood, and that is the best, the best, the best.

Sometimes, though, the things that go on between girls aren't "just a normal part of growing up," as some people will tell you. Sometimes hurtful words and actions are meant to make a girl feel horrible about herself. Have you heard girls say things like this?

* You can't sit here. This seat's taken.
* Didn't you already wear that outfit this week?
* I'm gonna tell her she can't come to my sleepover after all. I just don't like her anymore.
* My mom's making me invite her, but we're all going to just ignore her.
* Haven't you ever heard of deodorant?

* If you keep hanging out with her, none of us will be your friends anymore.
* I heard — from a reliable source — that's she's already kissed a guy.
* Hey, girls, look who ate an entire *village* this summer!

When a girl says or does things on purpose to be hurtful and take away another girl's power to be herself — and she does it on a regular basis (like, it's practically her career) — that's called *bullying*. It *isn't* normal, and it doesn't have to be part of growing up. We'll talk tons about girl bullying later, but first, let's focus on what it takes for friendship to bounce you out of bed, sing you through the day, and make your dreams happy. Start by checking out your own closest girl relationship.

That Is SO Me

Read each sentence beginning below and then circle the sentence ending that is most true for you. Be totally honest so you can learn the most about yourself and your BFF.

1. I'm honest with my friend
   a. no matter what.
   b. unless she might think I'm lame.
   c. unless I know she'll get mad at me.
   d. when she's clueless.

2. When my friend and I have problems, I
   a. always talk to her about them.
   b. figure it's probably my fault and try to fix myself.
   c. don't bring it up because she might not be my friend anymore.
   d. tell other people what she's doing that I can't stand.

3. When my friend and I are WAY getting along, I
   a. tell her how cool she is.
   b. smile to myself and hope it keeps up.
   c. don't say anything because I might jinx it.
   d. tell her this is the way it has to be all the time or I'm out of there.

4. When my friend has something to tell me, I
   a. listen the way she listens to me.
   b. think about what I'm going to say when she's through that's just as cool.
   c. don't say anything while she's talking, because she'd cut me off anyway.
   d. listen until it starts driving me nuts.

continued on next page

5. When my friend is upset, I
   a. do what she needs me to do (let her cry, bring her cookies, give her a hug, whatever I know works for her).
   b. am always afraid I'm going to say something stupid.
   c. agree with whatever she says so she won't get upset at *me*.
   d. give her advice as soon as I get what she's talking about (or she'll go on for days).

6. If somebody's being mean to my friend, I
   a. stand up for her.
   b. tell her I would never be mean to her.
   c. be extra careful not to be mean to her myself.
   d. take care of it for her because she's kind of a wimp when it comes to stuff like that.

7. If something way cool happens to me, I
   a. can't wait to tell my friend, because it's even cooler when she squeals with me.
   b. wonder if my friend is going to think it's as cool as I do.
   c. try not to make it sound as cool as it is so my friend doesn't get jealous that it didn't happen to her.
   d. tell my friend right away because she's always trying to be cooler than me (and I hate that).

8. If my friend tells me a secret and I promise not to tell, I
   a. keep it to myself because she trusts me.
   b. only tell people I trust who I want to be friends with too.
   c. don't tell anybody because if I did and she found out, she would totally hate me forever.
   d. only tell other people if she does something that makes me mad.

9. When my friend does something, well, lame, I
   a. laugh with her so she doesn't feel stupid.
   b. wait to see how she feels about it and then do the same (laugh, cry, hide my head in a bag).
   c. pretend I didn't notice so she doesn't take her embarrassment out on me.
   d. laugh my head off because she's such a klutz all the time!

10. I think my friend will always be there
    a. because we treat each other super well.
    b. if I can be as cool as she is.
    c. if she doesn't get mad at me.
    d. because she knows she needs me.

To understand what your answers mean, write the letter for the answer you gave to each of the questions next to the number. (You'll notice that they're in groups instead of in order.)

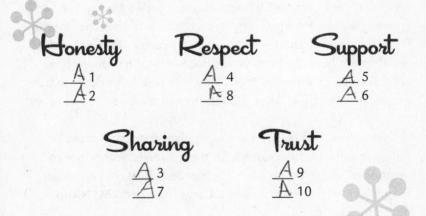

Honesty
A 1
A 2

Respect
A 4
A 8

Support
A 5
A 6

Sharing
A 3
A 7

Trust
A 9
A 10

Your A answers tell you that you're the kind of friend every girl wants for her BFF in the areas of honesty, respect, support, sharing, and trust. Yeah, baby, you basically know how to be a great pal when it comes to those things. Now look at your **b**, **c**, and **d** answers, because those are your challenges for being the best friend in every way. You're up for it!

Your B answers show you in what areas you tend to let your friend make the decisions about your friendship. It's good to take other people's feelings into consideration, but you need to be your true self as well. This book will help you feel more confident about being honest, confronting problems, and just relaxing and being authentic with your girlfriends. You'll find out that you are SO worth being friends with.

Your C answers help you see in what ways you're somewhat afraid of your friend. Will she be mad at you? Will she think you're stupid? Will she get jealous? Will she dump you? In a real friendship, both girls are equal. This book will help you work on those things with your BFF — or guide you in finding other friends who don't expect you to tiptoe around them.

Your D answers mean that, in those friendship areas, you don't really respect your BFF and may be hurting her without even knowing it. No friend gets to be the boss of the other, or the friendship will fall apart — and it won't be pretty. Rather than stay in that place, you can learn in this book how to be your strong, confident, go-getter self without knocking your buds down in the process. Once you do, your friendships will rock.

Jesus obviously believed in having great friends, because he hung around with twelve of his for three straight years — not to mention all the other people he befriended along the way: Mary Magdalene; Mary, Martha, and Lazarus from Bethany; Nicodemus; and Zacchaeus.

Jesus didn't just party at weddings and go on boat rides with them. He was constantly talking to them about how to treat each other. Things like:

> "You're blessed when you care. At the moment of being 'care-full,' you find yourselves cared for."
>
> —Matthew 5:7 (*The Message*)

> "If you enter your place of worship and, about to make an offering, you suddenly remember a grudge a friend has against you, abandon your offering, leave immediately, go to this friend and make things right."
>
> —Matthew 5:23-24 (*The Message*)

> "Ask yourself what you want people to do for you, then ... do it for them."
>
> —Matthew 7:12 (*The Message*)

In this book you're going to read a lot more of what Jesus said about friendships, because the gospel is all *about* our relationships, not only with God, but with other people—both the ones we like and the ones we aren't so crazy about. Who knew that the Bible could be your total guide to ALL the stuff that goes on with girls? So let's get started with a summary of what a truly amazing friendship is like.

Here's the Deal

Paul of Tarsus was a special teacher God used to show people how to totally live life like Jesus the Christ. In one of his letters to a group of folks who were obviously struggling with their relationships, he gave a summary of what true friendship is. He used the word *love* in 1 Corinthians 13. Think of the word *friendship* in place of *love* so you'll really see how this applies to you and your BFF or group of close girlfriends.

True friendship

* *never gives up.* It's never too much trouble to work out problems. Friends hang in there because they love each other.
* *cares more for others than for self.* It's important for each person to say what she wants and needs, but it's even more important to find out what's going on with the other person. It just isn't that much fun to always be on top when everybody else is miserable.
* *doesn't want what it doesn't have.* Real friends love each other for who they are. They help each other become their best selves, instead of trying to do total personality makeovers on their friends.
* *doesn't strut, doesn't have a swelled head, doesn't force itself on others, isn't always "me first."* True friendship means everyone is equal, with nobody trying to be the boss.
* *doesn't fly off the handle.* Good friends may get annoyed with each other (ya think?) or even mad sometimes. But instead of pitching fits, they calm down, talk things through, and come through it with a stronger friendship.
* *doesn't keep score of the sins of others.* Both people in a friendship are going to make mistakes. They forgive, they make things better, and they move on.

* *doesn't revel when others grovel.* No real friend is ever going to be happy when her BFF feels rotten in the friendship because it's lopsided. Friends share their hurts and comfort each other.
* *takes pleasure in the flowering of truth.* In a great friendship, who cares who's right and who's wrong as long as arguments are settled and decisions are made that are good for everyone? BFFs focus on what's good and real — and fun!
* *trusts God always.* Forever Friends realize that their coming together is a gift from God. They pray together and for each other. They talk about what God wants them to do in tough situations. They know something good is going to come out of everything they go through together.
* *always looks for the best.* One friend chooses another because she's fabulous. Why pick her apart? The best buds, the ones who last, see the best stuff in each other and say it. Out loud. A lot.

That's what a true friendship looks like. If that doesn't describe yours right now, don't decide you're a loser. Relationships can be hard, but they're so worth it. Ready to find out how you can get there? Let's go!

You're Good to Go

Since this book is about getting along with *other girls,* you obviously won't learn the most from it by doing it all by yourself. Hopefully your BFF or your group of close buds will want to learn with you so your friendship will rock. This is the place to share this book with her (or them) and do some fun stuff together.

What if you don't have close girlfriends? Maybe you just moved to a new town or school, or none of your old girlfriends are in your class anymore. Or perhaps you've always been kind of a loner or have had trouble finding girls you really want to connect with. Think of at least one person you know that you'd like to spend time with and who has shown interest in being your friend too. Right now, with this book in your hand, is the perfect opportunity to start a brand-new friendship and grow it well from the very beginning. Take it step by step. God's in the middle of it with you.

What you'll need:

* ❀ Your best friend, your small group of close friends (not, like, every girl in your whole class!) or one or two girls you'd like to be friends with.
* ❀ This book. It would be neat if you all had your own copies, but sharing is fun too.
* ❀ Paper and fun pens or markers. If you really want to go crazy, bring on the glitter, stickers, and other cool art stuff.
* ❀ A place to get together where you can all write — like a table or snack bar or the floor of your room — and where you won't be interrupted while you're doing important friend work. Ask your mom to help with that part if you have brothers and sisters. Moms know about girlfriend stuff.

What to do:

Share what you've learned in this chapter and ask if your friends want to have an even better friendship than you already have—or if they'd like to start a friendship with you. The answer will probably be yes, but if it isn't, pick someone else!

Turn back to the friendship qualities in "Here's the Deal." Talk about how your friendship is doing on each point. You can even give yourselves a score or a grade if that's your thing, but just writing down the areas where your BFF-ness needs the most work is fine.

Using your art supplies, each of you can write out and decorate a beautiful pledge for making your friendship the best it can be. "Here's the Deal" will get you started, but feel free to add your own ideas too.

What it tells you:

+ That you already know a lot about being a good friend.
+ That being friends gets easier and is a whole lot more fun when you're in it together.
+ That your friends want the same thing you want—a friendship that rocks!
+ That the best is yet to come.

That's What I'm Talkin' About!

After your meeting—and maybe even in the days ahead—write, draw, or doodle your responses to what happened and continues to happen.

The best thing about when we got together was

Our biggest challenge as friends is

When I think about the times ahead with my friend/friends, I feel

chapter two

Closed Cliques ...
OR SISTER CHICKS?

For the rest of the morning, Emily couldn't concentrate on anything except Lara:

Lara helping Katy with her math, instead of doing the problems with *her*.

Lara going to the girls' restroom with Katy and the Price Tags instead of with her and Kimberly and Mary Elizabeth.

Lara letting Katy pull her away when Emily went up to her at the water fountain.

By the time the class went outside for PE, Emily was sure she was going to be sick soon. Coach let her sit out the volleyball game. She sat on the walk, leaned against the cold brick wall, and thought hard.

Just last Saturday, things had been so different ...

The four Fab Friends as they called themselves — Emily, Lara, Mary Elizabeth, and Kimberly — had been at The Yellow House celebrating Emily's birthday. It was the best place on the planet for a girl party. While the moms had their tea in a separate room, the Fab Friends were served at a special table, like they were grown-ups.

"This is what we're going to be like when we're adults," Emily said. She offered a toast with her hot chocolate-filled china cup.

Lara giggled. "Only we'll be taller."

"And all be wearing bras," Mary Elizabeth said.

Kimberly choked on the pink cookie she'd just taken a bite of.

"We can talk about anything," Emily said. "None of us ever tells each other's secrets to anybody, right?"

They all nodded and slipped for a minute into happy silence.

"Hey, you guys," Lara said, "would it be okay if I invited that new girl — "

"Tia?" Emily said.

"Yeah. I want to ask her to my sleepover."

"You don't have to have our permission," Emily said.

"Bring her on!" Mary Elizabeth flung her arms up, almost sending Kimberly's black cherry soda into flight.

Lara giggled. "You are my favorite klutz, M.E."

"I try," Mary Elizabeth said.

Emily grinned around the table. "This is perfect."

"Well, it *was*." Kimberly glared toward the door, and Emily groaned inside. Katy and her Price Tag Girls were fluttering in like a swarm of glossy-lipped butterflies. Katy, of course, led the way to a table in the corner that was frilled up in hot pink. Her friends flitted around her, nudging each other aside to get the seat next to her.

Mary Elizabeth rolled her eyes.

"I hope they don't start picking on us," Kimberly said.

"Don't worry," Emily grunted. "They won't even notice we're here."

"Right," Lara said. "We're not in the clique." She tilted her head. "Did you ever wonder what it would be like to be friends with them?"

Mary Elizabeth sniffed. "It doesn't look like that much fun to me."

She was right, Emily decided.

"Kelsey, quit playing with the spoon," she heard Katy say. "It's annoying."

Another girl giggled. Katy narrowed her eyes at her.

It seemed that nobody on Katy's left was on her approval list today. What kind of friend was she if you had to be measuring up all the time?

As if somebody had shouted a command, the Price Tag Girls leaned into the table, heads bent over the pink tea set. One of the girls on Katy's right whispered, eyes wide, hands shaping the secret story she was obviously telling. Everyone else seemed to cling to her every word as if it were a life preserver.

"They're gossiping," Mary Elizabeth said without really moving her lips.

"They're *always* gossiping," Kimberly whispered.

Emily looked at Lara, and then they ripped open into giggles.

"What?" Mary Elizabeth said.

"We're gossiping about *them* right *now*!" Emily said.

They all pointed their heads close together and whispered like a chorus: "Just because it's true doesn't mean we have to say it."

It felt so good to be friends at that exact moment. Emily had been sure it was the best birthday present ever.

Now she looked miserably at the volleyball court. Lara held the ball, ready to serve, and Emily waited for her to pound it over the net. She was the best player in the entire class, even better than the boys.

Just as Lara raised her arm, Katy hissed at her from the sideline where she was ready to rotate in. Lara waited as Katy hurried over to her and whispered between hands cupped around Lara's ear. Emily felt as if she were being stabbed.

Lara clearly had a question mark on her face. Katy poked her in the arm with her knuckle and said, "Just do it."

Whatever it is, don't *do it, Lara,* Emily wanted to cry out.

Lara tossed the ball up, gave it a hard smack, and then hid her face in her hands. But Emily watched, mouth hanging open, as the ball bonked another Price Tag right in the back of the head.

In the midst of Coach blasting the whistle and girls shrieking and boys yelling, "Score," Emily saw Katy bounce to Lara and high-five her. Sweet Lara, who wouldn't even kill a mosquito, high-fived her back.

At least, she *thought* it was Lara. But in that moment, she looked like someone Emily didn't even know.

That Is SO Me

Just as Emily looked at her relationship with the Fab Friends, think about how your group of close buds works together. Consider each friend-group behavior on the left side of the page. Then place a star (*) under the heading that best describes your group. Remember to be totally honest. (After all, nobody's friendships are perfect.)

In My Friend Group We ...	Not in a Million Years	Sometimes	Totally
push a girl out if we get tired of her.	*	☐	☐
stick together against the rest of the school world.	☐	☐	*
invite another girl in ONLY if she's exactly like us.	*	☐	☐
have rules we follow to stay in the group.	☐	*	☐
have a leader who's in charge.	*	☐	☐

	Not in a Million Years	Sometimes	Totally
have fights and get back together.	✸	❑	❑
take sides among ourselves.	❑	✸	❑
show weird people how weird they are.	✸	❑	❑
decide what's cool to do, wear, and say—and all do, wear, and say those things.	✸	❑	❑
have a lunch table nobody but us sits at.	❑	❑	❑
run things at our school or in our class.	✸	❑	❑
say whatever we want about people.	❑	✸	❑
Count the stars in each column.	7	3	1

Read about your group—the column with the most stars.

Not in a Million Years

Although you have a group of close friends who have stuff in common and value the same things and may even act a lot alike, you definitely have more of a sisterhood than a clique. Keep reading this chapter so you can make absolutely certain you never enter closed clique-dom.

Your group of best buds qualifies as a healthy sisterhood ... most of the time. But like all friends, you do have things you could be doing that are kinder and more open to the girls you aren't as close to. This chapter will help you move right into the Sister Chick column.

Sometimes

You and your friends may have moved into clique-hood, which means you're probably missing out on a lot. And you could even be hurting other people outside your group, possibly without even knowing it. Read this chapter really carefully and be ready for some changes that will make you, your girlfriends, and the other girls you know a whole bunch happier.

Let's talk about the Clique Trick

What it is:

A clique forms when a group of girls becomes a closed club that has no room for anybody new. It's usually led by one girl who's put herself in charge of deciding who's in and who's out and what's cool and what's not. You can spot a clique by looking for these kinds of things:

- ❁ It acts like it's a better friend group than any other.
- ❁ The girls in it base their worth on being accepted by the other girls in the group (not on being kind, fun people).
- ❁ A girl has to earn her way in.
- ❁ A girl could be booted out at any time.

Unfortunately, there are even cliques of Christian girls. How un-Christlike is that?

What it looks like:

Nicole: Do you guys mind if I sit at your table?
Michelle: Actually, this is a private table.
Michelle's Friend: There's no room anyway.

Nicole: This chair's empty.
Michelle's Other Friend: No, she means there's no room for YOU.
Michelle: No offense, but are you, like, slow or something?
We already told you this on the bus ... at recess ...
Michelle's Friend: Are you special ed?
Michelle's Other Friend: (giggle, giggle)

What it isn't:

A healthy friend group, which

 * is based on really liking each other and enjoying the same things;
 * is always open to finding new people to be friends with them; and
 * doesn't label other girls but finds out who they really are.

Why girls join cliques:

Often cliques are made up of "popular" girls that everyone else either likes or envies. Being close to the cool girls makes them feel cool too.

A clique can sometimes turn on an "outsider" and make her life miserable. (We'll talk more about that in chapter 5.) Sometimes girls work their way into cliques to protect themselves from being targets.

A clique can look like fun from the outside: a group of girls always together, knowing where they belong at all times, and being secure that there will always be somebody there. But once they're "in," some girls will stop acting like themselves and try to be more like the other girls in the clique—just to hold on to that safety they think they have there.

What happens as a result:

The "outsiders"

* are targets for teasing and really hurtful stuff cliques sometimes do.
* can feel like they're not worth as much (especially when a clique-type girl whines, "Do I have to work with *her*?")
* are often excluded from parties and sleepovers, simply because they aren't "in."
* may get so hurt they become mean themselves, spreading rumors, giving hateful looks, even giving back the same kind of cruelty they're getting.

The "insiders"

✪ can get a false idea that they really are better than everyone else.
✪ sometimes bully outsiders just to keep up that feeling (more in chapter 5).
✪ are closed off from making new friends who aren't willing to be just like them.
✪ aren't allowed to be independent and make their own choices in things like clothes or activities for fear *they'll* be excluded.
✪ can be so afraid of losing their place in the clique, they feel they can't afford to be nice to less "popular" kids.
✪ may not be happy. There may be so much drama in the clique, it gets crazy; her friends don't make her happy— they just make her feel "in."

(Important Thing)

Be careful not to assume that just because a girl is "popular," she must be a snob, or that a group of friends who are all well-liked are naturally a mean clique. Is that "leader girl" fun and outgoing? A hard worker in school? Does she help people feel good about themselves? Is she understanding? Can she take charge without being bossy? Does she seem confident? If the answer is yes, that's why everyone likes her. Think of her as a kid just like you. Smile. Ask friendly questions like, "Where did you get those cute flip-flops?" Be your fun self around her. You might make a new friend. Of course, if a girl who is the center of everything is making meanness to you her full-time career, avoid her group. If she snubs you, shrug it off. She's missed a great opportunity to get to know fabulous you.

GOT GOD?

Jesus was definitely popular. Ya think? People climbed trees, hiked up mountains, and had themselves lowered through roofs to be near him!

Jesus and his disciples were not a clique, even though they were the closest ones to him, and he was clearly the leader.

He healed the leper, the worst outcast you could imagine (Matthew 8:1–4), not to mention people who were possessed by demons—not the people most often invited to parties (Matthew 8:16 and 28–32)—as well as a woman who'd been married a bajillion (five) times and who no guy worried about his popularity would even speak to (John 4:1–30). He even did it right in front of the Pharisee clique.

When he heard that the Pharisees' clique was talking smack about him, he didn't lead his friends in some plan to get back at them (Matthew 15:12–14). In fact he was open and honest with them every time he talked to them (all through the Gospels). Luke 14:1–24 is a good example.

He even included little kids, in spite of the disciples trying to run them off (Matthew 19:13–15).

He warned his disciples about being friends with people who loaded them down with rules they couldn't possibly keep all the time. He told them not to set people up as experts over their lives, but save that authority for God (Luke 12:4–5).

One of the disciples wanted to stop a man who was driving out demons in Jesus' name—just because the man wasn't in their group. Jesus wouldn't let him stop the man (Mark 9:38–40).

Jesus was just the kind of friend God had predicted he would be:

- ✧ He won't yell, won't raise his voice;
- ✧ there'll be no commotion....
- ✧ He won't walk over anyone's feelings,
- ✧ won't push you into a corner.

—Matthew 12:19–20 (*The Message*)

To be a follower of Christ means to try to be as much like Jesus as we can, especially in our friendships. Pray that God will guide you to be part of a sisterhood that stays out of clique-dom—for good!

A girl with the label "popular" could be under a lot of pressure to appear perfect. A lot of girls in that category say they feel like they can never have an off day. They get exhausted trying to juggle so many friendships or be in charge of so many people. Often, they're afraid to try anything "different," like learn to knit or do fifty cart-wheels across the lawn because it feels good. Pray for any girls you can see who are in that position, even if they're mean to you. It's hard to hate someone you talk to God about every day.

Here's the Deal

You may not be able to stamp out cliques forever, but you can make sure your own friend group doesn't become one. You can try these things:

* Be connected by a very real love for each other, not just by the yearning to be in the popular group.

* Have things in common but still be individuals, each making your own decisions about what to wear and how to talk and what activities to be in.
* Beware if one girl in your friend group starts to act as boss of all of you; remind her that you are all equals.
* Refuse to make demands of each other or threaten to kick someone out because she doesn't do absolutely everything the group tells her to. There's a difference between sharing the same basic ideas, and being identical twins, triplets, or quadruplets!
* Refuse to gossip about other girls, especially the girls in the clique. If you bad-mouth them, how are you any different from them?
* Stay open to making new friends. Instead of excluding, include; be friendly and kind to girls who don't seem to have any buddies at all. Even be warm toward clique members, who are probably really great girls inside — just a little confused right now.

What it looks like:

Kathryn: Hi, Nicole. Wanna sit with us?

Nicole: Are you sure?

Kathryn's Friend: Why wouldn't we be sure?

Nicole: Michelle and them wouldn't let me sit at their table . . .

Kathryn's Other Friend: Their loss. Want a cookie?

You're Good to Go

Get your BFF or girlfriend group together again and take a good hard look at this clique thing.

What you'll need:

+ this book
+ honesty

What to do:

◎ Turn to "That Is SO Me" in this chapter and do the "quiz" together.

◎ Talk over your answers until everyone (or the two of you) agree.

◎ If you're just becoming friends with the girls you invite over, do the quiz thinking about what you all want your friend group to be like.

◎ If your pals are not the type to sit around talking for more than about seven seconds, try acting out each item before you all decide on it.

What it tells you:

✝ Whether you all see your friendship the same way.

✝ Where you can celebrate your sisterhood.

✝ What things you'll want to change in your friendship so you don't hurt other people, or yourself.

What to do now:

Pay careful attention to those things that take you to the edge of cliquey-ness and enjoy making your circle of friends a real sisterhood (with the help of the rest of this book!).

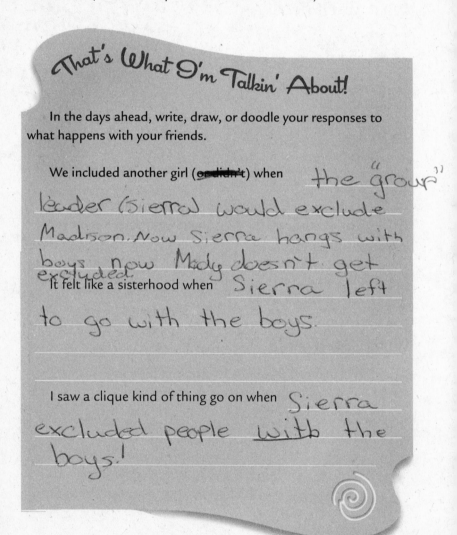

That's What I'm Talkin' About!

In the days ahead, write, draw, or doodle your responses to what happens with your friends.

We included another girl (~~or didn't~~) when the "group" leader (Sierra) would exclude Madison. Now Sierra hangs with boys, now Mady doesn't get excluded.

It felt like a sisterhood when Sierra left to go with the boys.

I saw a clique kind of thing go on when Sierra excluded people with the boys!

chapter three

Friendship
FLUBS

At lunchtime, Emily watched Katy Cuthbert lead her group across the cafeteria like a queen with an adoring flock of handmaidens. And there was Lara, right behind her, eyes round and impressed-looking as Katy tossed words at her over her shoulder.

"That is just wrong," Mary Elizabeth said, close to Emily's ear.

"Totally." Kimberly bit a hunk out of her pizza slice and talked on with her mouth full. "I still say we don't speak to Lara until she comes to her senses."

Mary Elizabeth nodded. "And even then, I still think we should make her work to get back in with us."

Emily picked a pepperoni off her own slice and tossed it onto the paper plate. "I can't do it," she said. "I just can't be evil to her."

"After the way she dumped us this morning?" Mary Elizabeth shook her head. "If you go running after her now, she'll just do it again. Trust me."

Emily used to think she could trust Lara. And she had to find out if she still could.

She wiped her hands on the back of her jeans and headed toward Katy's table — a place one dared not go unless invited.

"You're gonna be sor-ry," Mary Elizabeth said in a sing-song voice.

But Emily couldn't believe that. She and Lara had been best friends since second grade. She would never make Emily "sorry" for *talking* to her. Hello-o.

One of the Price Tag Girls nudged Katy as Emily approached the table. Katy's lip curled into an unattractive smile. Emily wondered if she smelled something bad.

"What?" Katy said.

"I need to talk to Lara."

"Oh." Katy looked across the table at Lara, who was nibbling the corner of a Wheat Thin. "Do you want to talk to this ... person?"

She might as well have said "this insect." Emily looked quickly at Lara, but her best friend was examining her cracker as if it too might be some kind of bug.

"Either talk to her or tell her to go away," Katy said to Lara.

Lara looked up, and for a horrid moment, Emily thought she was going to shoo her off. But she slowly pushed her chair back and stood up. Emily grabbed her by the sleeve and dragged her several feet from Katy. The P.T.s leaned so far in their direction, Emily thought the table would tip over. At least, she *hoped* it would.

"*What* is going on?" Emily said.

"What do you mean?" Lara said.

"Hello-o! You haven't talked to me all morning. You're hanging out with Katy — who we can't stand ..."

"She's actually nice when you get to know her."

Emily stared. Lara, on the other hand, was looking everywhere but at her.

"This is too weird," Emily said. "You always eat lunch with us."

Lara's gaze drifted to the floor. "We're talking about the social studies project."

"So how come you're in her group instead of with us? We always work together."

"Well ... maybe we don't have to, like, do absolutely everything together."

"Why *not?*"

Lara hugged her folded arms against herself and hunched her shoulders.

"What?" Emily said.

"Katy told me some things that people have been saying about us."

"Like what?"

"I can't tell you."

"I'm your best friend!"

"You okay, Lara?" Katy called from the table.

Lara looked back at her. Katy smiled, sweet as the sour cream and onion potato chip poised between her manicured fingers. Lara straightened her shoulders and finally met Emily's eyes. The way she narrowed them gave Emily a chill.

"You already *know,*" Lara said. "You just won't admit it. And you know what? You're not the boss of me. I'll sit wherever I want, with whoever I want."

Lara gave her hair a toss, just the way Katy always did. The way they had always made fun of in private.

"Share my chips," Emily heard Katy say as Lara slipped back into her chair.

Lara held out her hand, and Emily exploded. *"I'm* not the boss of you ... but you're gonna let *her* be the boss of you?" She heard her own voice screech above the sudden cafeteria hush as she finished with, "You *hate* onion potato chips!"

And then, with everyone gaping at her, Emily ran for the nearest exit.

Here's the Deal

You're probably feeling pretty bad for Emily right now. And you might even have some sympathy for Lara, who is also in a tough place. (Katy, not so much, but we'll talk about her in chapter 5.) The reason you can almost feel what they're going through is because most girls between the ages of eight and twelve experience some of the same things.

Most of the time a girl commits a "friendship flub" for one of these reasons:

✿ She feels like she's not important, and she wants to feel she is.
✿ She feels bad about herself, and she wants to feel better.
✿ She's afraid she doesn't belong, and she so wants to.
✿ She's bored, and she wants to stir things up.
✿ She doesn't always know how to treat people, but she wants to.
✿ She doesn't quite know who she is yet, but she's trying.

None of those are about someone just being a loser as a friend, which means most mistakes made in girl groups can be worked out. Let's look at seven "friendship flubs" and see how to fix them.

#1 Friendship Flub: The Rumor Tumor

What it looks like:

It starts something like this:
"I heard—from somebody who really knows—that she ..."
"I don't know if this is true, but I kinda think it is: She ..."
"Okay, A told me that B told her that she actually saw C ..."
"You are not going to believe what's going around about ..."

What it is:

As soon as those words are out of somebody's mouth, everyone else is leaning in — eyes wide, ears even wider — ready to hear the latest gossip. This may be the second, third, or even fourth time the story's been told, but you can bet that each time it has gotten a little bit juicier, just a tad longer, and probably a whole lot more false.

What it isn't:

* News. Real news is actually true ...
* Something told out of concern for the person being talked about. If the teller were really concerned, she'd be talking to the person herself, not everybody else on the planet.

What happens because of it:

* Lies are spread. Never a good thing.
* The person being gossiped about gets her feelings hurt.
* Some people believe the rumor is true, and the girl they talk about gets a reputation she doesn't deserve.
* Girls have actually had to *change schools* because of rumors spread about them — by their own friends.

How to fix it:

Find out if the "news" is true. Go straight to the person being talked about and ask her. Or just use common sense. Some things are so obviously false they're ridiculous. EXAMPLE: "Madison's mother has been married sixteen times." Oh, come on ...

If the answer is no, it isn't true, then simply STOP IT right there. Don't breathe a word of it to anyone, and encourage the gossipers to do the same. Start a new topic of conversation. Stand on your head if you need to but do whatever it takes to snuff that rumor out. EXAMPLE: Everybody is saying Allison made all F's in the last school she went to. It just isn't true. Wouldn't it be awful for Allison if that got around?

If the rumor is true, ask yourself: Will it help the person being talked about if I tell this to someone else?

If the answer is no, it won't help her, STOP IT right there. So what if it's true. If it could hurt her, embarrass her, or betray her trust, it is just NOT okay to spread it any further. Change the subject and move on. EXAMPLE: Taylor has six toes on her left foot. You know it for a fact. But what good is it going to do Taylor for you to tell everybody? It would probably embarrass her, and there's sure to be some absurd little boy who would call her a freak right in the cafeteria.

If the answer is yes, it would help her if you told someone, then tell the RIGHT PERSON, usually an adult you can trust with the information. EXAMPLE: Ashley throws her lunch away every day because she says she's getting fat — and she's, like, skinny as a pencil. If she won't get help when you tell her she should, go to the counselor yourself, or tell your mom, who can talk to her mom. You and your friends can't fix this for Ashley.

To make that easier to remember, follow this diagram for healing the Rumor Tumor:

Rumor

is it true?

yes

no

hurtful

helpful

STOP it.

STOP it.

tell the right person

Remember that if people gossip to you, they'll probably also gossip about you. A person who gossips can't keep a secret. So don't be the person who can't be trusted. Don't start gossip, don't listen to it, and don't repeat it. There are more fun and important things to talk about.

#2 Friendship Flub:
The Boots and the Doormat

What it is:

One friend always gets her way. She's so ... well, bossy, her pals won't argue with her. After a while, they just assume her way is the only way—which is fine with her!

What it looks like:

Elizabeth: Hey, Sarah, you want to do something? Hang out?
Sarah: Yeah. Turn on the TV and get us some chips.
Elizabeth: Oh. Okay. Whatever you want to do is fine with me.

Imagine Sarah with an in-charge voice and a pointing finger, and you've got The Boots who walks all over her friends and might not even know she's doing it. Give Elizabeth a tiny voice and shrugging shoulders, and you're imagining The Doormat who won't stand up to The Boots and doesn't know she can.

What it isn't:

- ◎ One friend just naturally being stronger than the other. Hello-o! Friendship is for equals. This is not mother and daughter or boss and employee or master and slave. We're talking friends here!
- ◎ One friend making all the decisions because the other friend will never speak up. She probably never says what she wants because she's never asked. Or maybe she's tried and been told, "Nah. That's lame."

What happens because of it:

Both The Boots and The Doormat can end up feeling resentful after a while.

Boots

- ✳ may get tired of making all the decisions without ever being challenged;
- ✳ might get so sick of her friend acting "wimpy" she treats her even more harshly to get her to explode; or
- ✳ might be annoyed if Doormat does speak up for something she wants, because the decisions have always been *her* job.

Doormat

* will probably get irritated never having what she wants, but she will more than likely keep that to herself,
* until she bursts out in anger, making Boots mad,
* or goes off and finds other friends she might do the same thing with.

How to fix it:

The Boots and the Doormat can have a friendship on equal terms if each of them becomes *assertive*. That means

* saying what she wants, needs, or thinks in a firm, polite way;
* always showing respect when she speaks her mind;
* listening to the other person's wants and needs; and
* making a decision together.

What it looks like:

Elizabeth: Hey, Sarah. You want to do something? Hang out?
Sarah: Sure. I'm thinking TV and some chips. What are you thinking?
Elizabeth: I'm thinking the chips sound good, but what if we watched a movie instead? I'm sort of sick of TV.
Sarah: Sweet. Whatcha got?

See the dif? Both friends keep the power to be themselves, but they don't *use* that power *over* each other. Yes! Sweet!

#3 Friendship Flub:
The Mind-Reading Game

What it is:

When friends expect each other to know what they're thinking and feeling without having to say anything. It's as if being best friends means you can see into each other's brains.

What it looks like:

Brianna: Are you mad at me?
Hannah: Du-uh. It's about time you figured that out.
Brianna: Why? What did I do?
Hannah: You *know* what you did.
Brianna: Nu-uh! Honest!
Hannah: Well, you *should* know.
Brianna: How would I—
Hannah: Because we're best *friends!* Only, if you're gonna do stuff like this, maybe we're not.

What it isn't:

+ an expectation anybody should have, even of her best friend;
+ a sign of being super close; it's more a sign of being afraid to come right out and say what's making her mad or upset; or
+ a reason to stop being friends; even people who have been *married* for twenty years don't know what their partners are thinking all the time.

What happens:

☆ Friends make big holes in their friendships instead of talking things out.

☆ One person tells every other girl in the class what's bothering her about her friend, instead of going to the BFF herself and working it through.

☆ Eventually somebody says, "Well, if you don't know, I'm sure not gonna tell you," and where does that get them?

How to fix it:

— Decide you're not going to expect your friend to know what's bothering you. When was the last time *you* read *her* mind?

— If your friend has upset you or hurt your feelings, be honest with her. You don't have to yell at her. Just calmly tell her how you feel and why.

— Definitely don't share your complaint about her with everybody in life. She's the only one who needs to hear about it, unless you want to first run it by your mom or another adult you trust.

— If your friend expects you to read *her* mind, remind her that's not one of your many talents, and assure her you're not going to freak out over what she has to say (and then, of course, *don't* freak out!).

— Make a pledge to each other that you will always try to work things out.

What it looks like:

Nicole: Are you mad at me?
Hannah: Yeah, kinda.

Nicole: I wish you woulda said something. What's up?

Hannah: When you told Tracy I was spoiled because I'm an only child, it made it sound like I'm a brat. I'm SO not!

Nicole: Yikes, I'm sorry. I was just kidding.

Hannah: It hurt my feelings, though.

Nicole: I'll never do it again, I promise.

Hannah: Do you really think I'm spoiled?

Nicole: No-o! I was just showing off. Do you hate me?

Hannah: Hello-o! You're my best friend!

#4 Friendship Flub: The Drama Queen

What it is:

A girl turns just about everything into cause for tears or screaming or all-out war. It doesn't even have to be over something big.

What it looks like:

Susan: (in a low voice) Um, Cara, you have a little booger coming out of your nose. You might wanna wipe it off.

Cara: Thanks for embarrassing me! You always do that!

Jenny: Lauren took Ashley to the mall Saturday instead of me, and I'm her best friend. I'm not speaking to her until she says she's sorry.

Grace: Then neither are we. We'll show her what it feels like to be left out.

Lydia: We were both gonna wear our pink hats today. Where's yours?

Hillary: Aw, man! I forgot it.

Lydia: No you didn't! You left it home on purpose!

Hillary: I didn't! Honest!

Lydia: If you didn't want to wear it, you coulda just told me. Now I feel like a total geek! Maybe we shouldn't even be best friends!

What it isn't:

* Some girls just being sensitive and emotional. Getting hurt feelings and crying is "just being sensitive." Having a total freak-out over something small is probably about some other issues that a grown-up could help with.
* Harmless. Hurtful things are often said during drama scenes that can't be un-said.
* Hormones out of control. Nah. Being a little weepier than usual could be from bouncing hormones, but we can't blame full-out blowups on puberty.

What happens because of it:

* Friends get pulled in so that a dramatic scene turns into a full-length, real-life play. Reality TV has nothing on the dramas girls can create!
* Friendships stop being fun since there's always an issue being cried over.
* Anger, fights, hysteria, and "breaking up/getting back together" become a habit. There's no room anymore for just doing normal friend things.
* Friendship makes life harder instead of easier. What's up with that?

How to fix it:

* Choose your battles. Laugh off tiny comments. Shrug away your friend's occasional bad day. Save your reactions for things that really matter.
* Before you do react to something, find out the facts first. Does she know you're sensitive about that subject? Did she invite that other girl to go someplace instead of you because her mom told her to? Rather than assuming she didn't sign up for softball because she doesn't want to be with you, ask if it's only that she just plain hates softball. Having all the information usually heads off a blowup.
* When you do have a good reason to be upset, don't wait until you're out of control. Be honest with your friend about why you're about to blow a gasket. Talk about how YOU feel, not about what SHE'S done.
* Even better, try to avoid getting upset in the first place by letting your friends know what kinds of things you're sensitive about. Just keep the list short!

Be really careful about teasing your friends, even though you're only doing it in fun. That can set off not only a Drama Queen, but any girl who's sensitive about something — and who isn't?! Your friend may laugh a few times when you tell her she's a klutz, but a steady diet of that is bound to make her wonder if she really is and resent you for pointing it out. Teasing is supposed to be fun for everybody involved. If it isn't, find something else to laugh about.

* If everything really does seem to drive you nuts, or if you discover you really enjoy tearful scenes and screaming fits, go to an adult you trust and talk about it.
* Remember that nobody's life is nonstop drama. A little bit of boring can be a relief!
* If you have a friend who always seems to be in the middle of a soap opera, let her know how you feel about her tragic performances at a time when she isn't putting one on. Tell her you love her and want to keep being friends, but you're not in it for the theatrics.
* Don't let her draw you into a production you don't really want a part in. Remove yourself from the situation or just say, "You know what? I think I'll stay out of this."

#5 Friendship Flub: The Green-Eyed Monster

What it is:

Plain old jealousy. One friend gets that pinched feeling when her BFF gets or does something better than what she has or does. It gets especially ugly when the jealous friend thinks *she* deserves it more than her friend.

What that looks like:

Danielle: Aren't you just so glad Amber won the talent contest?
Jenna: I guess.
Danielle: I thought she was your best friend.

Jenna: She is, which is why I know her mom totally coached her and made her costume and everything. I could've won too, if I had that much help.

What it isn't:

An okay thing just because it's human. Wanting to flush your little brother down the toilet is human too, but that doesn't mean you should go ahead and do it. No one is a horrible person for *feeling* jealous. It's what she does about it that makes the difference.

What happens because of it:

The Jealous One may

- be resentful. And just like in the case of Boots and Doormats, that causes all kinds of problems.
- feel guilty about wishing her best friend didn't have so many good things happening to her. When she feels bad about herself, it gets harder to feel good about anybody else.
- not be able to even congratulate her friend.
- talk trash about her friend to other people.

The Envied One may

- be hurt because her very best friend isn't happy for her.
- feel like she can't talk about her success to her friend, which is half the fun of having something good happen to her.
- try to back off on getting good grades or making more friends or whatever it is that's so great in her life, just so her friend won't feel bad.

get sick of having to practically apologize for doing well and start avoiding her otherwise fabulous friend.

How to fix it:

If you're jealous of a friend, try one of these:

✦ Admit, at least to yourself, that you're jealous. You aren't a horrible person. You just have something to work on (like every other person in the universe).

✦ Accept that everybody has both talents and flaws. So why sit around wishing you were perfect like her — when she isn't!

✦ Realize that jealousy, though human, doesn't make it okay for you to treat a friend badly. It isn't her fault she's a whiz kid in math or the next Mia Hamm in soccer.

✦ Turn your jealousy into a compliment. Tell her you're proud to be the BFF of the only straight-A student in the class, or the one with the longest hair, or whatever it is that you wish you could claim for yourself. It feels so much better to do that than to pout or put her down to the rest of the school.

✦ If she's done something really big (like winning the county spelling bee), throw a celebration for her — even if it's just the two of you sharing a huge cookie and a card you've made.

✦ Develop your own fabulous talents, not to compete with her, but to leave no room for wishing you were her. You'll be too happy just being you.

If your friend is jealous of you, try one of these:

✦ Don't let her think you and your life are perfect. Tell her about your fears and challenges — and jealous moments.

Then she won't look for chances to say, "Yes! She finally messed up!"

+ Compliment her on the very cool things *she* does. Tell her you think she rocks at drawing or can always give you the giggles.

+ Don't say, "Oh, you're just jealous," when she acts all funky. Sure, it's true, but saying that to her face will only make her feel worse. So will announcing it to your other friends. Try giving her some time. She'll probably be just fine.

+ If jealousy totally comes between you, tell your friend you'd love it if she didn't get mad about your being in the gifted and talented program or your leading role in the play. After all, you can say, you don't give her the silent treatment because she can talk to just about anybody and always gets elected class president. Ask if the two of you can just support each other.

What it looks like:

Danielle: Aren't you just so glad Amber won the talent contest?

Jenna: Isn't that so cool?

Danielle: Is it hard, though, that your best friend got first and you got third?

Jenna: Are you kidding me? I'm making this gigantic congratulations banner for her after school. You wanna help?

Be careful about the friend who seems to think you are absolutely perfect, and thinks she isn't as good as you are. That might feel lovely for a while, but sooner or later she's bound to resent you, because she's probably suffering from a low opinion of herself. Make sure she knows you aren't perfect and that you two are equals.

#6 Friendship Flub: Cloning

What it is:

❀ The need to be totally alike in absolutely everything.

❀ Maybe one friend copies everything the other one does, right down to the snort when she laughs.

❀ Perhaps one friend gets mad when her BFF doesn't want to wear identical outfits, use the same slang, and be in all the same activities.

What it looks like:

Alissa: Don't forget soccer tryouts are this afternoon.
Jordan: I'm not trying out for soccer this year.
Alissa: Are you mad at me about something?
Jordan: No! I just really don't like soccer that much anymore. I'm taking some art classes after school.
Alissa: What am I supposed to do? It'll stink without you.
Jordan: We'll still be together all day at school.
Alissa: Best friends are supposed to do everything together. I hate this!

What it isn't:

What best friends owe each other. Even identical twins aren't alike in every single way.

What happens because of it:

✳ The girl who wants to clone can get so clingy she becomes Velcro Friend, and that may frustrate her BFF to the point of screaming, "Get off me!"
✳ One or both friends can cheat themselves out of expanding the friend group to include more very cool girls.
✳ The one who buys into cloning may not try new things or make her own decisions, which means she misses out.
✳ Friendships don't usually last when one girl hangs onto the other like a ball and chain, or neither of them can go to the pencil sharpener without her friend attached to her at the hip. Too much togetherness is going to suffocate somebody sooner or later.

How to fix it:

If you're a cloner, try one of these solutions:

* Show your friend that you admire her by complimenting her, rather than trying to be her mirror image.
* Look at the reasons she likes you enough to be your BFF. Are you funny? Loyal? A good listener? Focus on those great qualities in yourself. What you each bring to the friendship makes it work.

If you always feel afraid when your friend does something different than you, talk to an adult you trust. She may be able to help you respect and enjoy the differences instead of being frightened by them.

If you have a friend who wants to be your clone:

* Instead of asking her to knock it off, tell her what you admire about her.
* Without mentioning the copycat thing, have a talk about all the ways you two are different. Laugh about them. Tell her that you love what's not the same about her.

When you make plans that don't include her or make a different choice from hers, also set up a time for the two of you to get together later and share your experiences.

If she doesn't get it after some patient trying, tell her as lovingly as you can that your friendship can't work if she's going to keep stealing your identity. Hopefully, if you do all of the above, it won't come to that.

What it looks like:

Alissa: Don't forget soccer tryouts are this afternoon.

Jordan: I totally forgot to tell you. I'm not trying out for soccer this year.

Alissa: Are you serious?

Jordan: Yeah, I just really don't like soccer that much anymore, you know?

Alissa: I guess you never did love it the way I do.

Jordan: Anyway, I'm taking some art classes after school.

Alissa: That's awesome. Your drawing totally rocks. I'll miss
you, though.

Jordan: We'll call each other when we get home.

Alissa: I can't wait to hear about it.

#7 Friendship Flub: Worthless Words

What it is:

- ✪ Anytime friends use words in a way that does nobody any good.
- ✪ Making promises they don't keep.
- ✪ Telling secrets they swore they wouldn't.
- ✪ Complaining to each other 24/7.
- ✪ Exaggerating the truth to make a better story.
- ✪ Saying things that are true, but would have been better left unsaid.
- ✪ Just plain old lying.

What it looks like:

Keisha swears she won't tell anyone else that Allie invited only her to go out on her grandpa's yacht—but she asks what she should bring in front of their other two friends.

Brenna's best friend Julia failed the last math test, and Brenna promises to help her before the next one. But the night before the test, she studies on her own.

Maddie wears the orange tights she loves to school. Her best friend, Britney, tells her she looks like she has carrots for legs and asks why she would put on something so ugly.

What happens because of it:

— A friend feels like she can't count on her BFF.
— She stops sharing her private thoughts with her friend.
— Both friends can become cranky and stop looking for the good in people and things.
— Both the lied-about and the lie-teller can forget what the truth really is and tell more and more whoppers.
— The friend who just can't keep her mouth shut gets a reputation for being the Blab Queen.

How to fix it:

✳ Make a pledge to each other to be careful with your words. Be specific about things that might be hard, like not spending all your time together gossiping about other people or not letting each other down with broken promises.

✳ When the temptation arises to spill a secret or make a critical (though funny!) remark, do whatever you have to do to zip your lips. Put your hand over your mouth. Leave the situation. Change the subject.

* If you just can't hold yourself back, let your friends know they can't share their secrets with you or trust that you'll come through on a promise. Ask them to help you with that.

* Before you make a promise, really think about whether you can keep it. Only say you'll do what you absolutely know you can deliver on.

Think about what you want people to say to and about you, and then say those things to and about your precious friends. Then they really will always be there.

What it looks like:

When their other friends ask what Allie and Keisha are doing this weekend, Keisha says, "What are *you* guys doing?"

When it's time for the math test, Brenna calls Julia and says, "I can only study together for an hour, but we can get a lot done."

When Maddie shows up at school in orange tights, Britney says, "So, did you watch *Hannah Montana* last night? It was SO good!"

That Is SO Me

You were probably thinking about your own friendships while you were reading, so now's a good time to zone in on how you and your friends are doing and what things you might want to work on.

How's Your Friendship Flubbiness?

Start at the beginning and follow the flow of your answers. Be honest!

Start

Your friend is absent from school and you know it's because of family problems. You ...

Don't tell anybody — even your cat.

Tell the popular girls because it's the first time they've paid attention to you.

Your BFF knows you know what's going on at your other friend's house and demands you share with her. You ...

Your friend comes back to school and won't talk to you. You ...

Ask her what's wrong and admit what you did.
go to 3 on page 65

Tell her you can't and switch the subject to her new kittens.
go to 1 on page 66

Are pretty sure it is because you told her secret but pretend to be clueless.
go to 2 on page 65

Tell her the whole story so she won't get mad at you.
go to 3 on page 65

2 Your friend tells your BFF, who tells you she's on your side. You ...

Say there are no sides.

Tell your BFF the friend is too sensitive and you don't want to be around her.

3 Your BFF tells you she's been invited to the friend's sleepover and asks if you were. You weren't. You ...

Tell her you hope she has a great time.
go to 1 below

Tell her you will be mad if she goes.

Your BFF says she wouldn't even think about doing anything with another friend if you don't. You ...

Say you think you two should have other friends too, even though she's your BFF.
go to 5 on page 66

Agree that you'll never do anything without checking with each other first.
go to 6 on page 66

1 Your BFF asks you to come over to see her kittens after school. You ...

Tell her you need to ask your mom.
go to 4 on page 66

Promise to come even though you haven't asked your mom.
go to 5 on page 66

4 You are almost flub free! You and your friends have your issues, but you work them out. Keep it up. Your sisterhood is precious.

5 There are some friendship flubs you wouldn't make if your stuffed animal collection depended on it. But sometimes, just like any friend, you make some not-so-friendly choices. Ask your friends to help you be the best bud you can be and do the same for them.

6 As fabulous a person as you are, it's hard for you to avoid the friendship flubs. Don't cheat your friends out of a super sisterhood with you. Work on your "flubbiness." Ask a grown-up for help. After all, you are great best-bud material.

GOT GOD?

Even Paul, who, remember, was one of God's most trusted teachers, was concerned about girl friendships. Check this out:

I urge Euodia and Syntyche to iron out their differences and make up. God doesn't want his children holding grudges. And, oh, yes, Syzygus, since you're right there to work things out, do your best with them.

– Philippians 4:2–3 (*The Message*)

Paul goes on to say that all three women are excellent Christians who have worked hard to get the message of Jesus to people. But they won't be able to do that if they're all tangled up in girl politics.

Leave it to God to show them — and us — how to make our friendships the best they can be. There are a lot of suggestions in "Here's the Deal" that you just read. God sums up in this one "fashion" passage. The parts in brackets are examples.

Dress in the wardrobe God picked out for you:
compassion [thinking about your friends' feelings, laughing with them, crying with them];
kindness [being there for your friends, bringing out the best in them rather than putting them down or cutting them out];
humility [not trying to be the boss, treating your friends as equals];
quiet strength [being willing to work things out without drama];
discipline [being trustworthy with secrets, keeping promises, being careful with your words].
Be even-tempered [choosing your battles, being assertive but not bossy];
content with second place [celebrating your friend's successes, cooperating instead of competing];
quick to forgive an offense. Forgive as quickly and completely as the Master forgave you [accepting that everyone has faults, talking problems through and letting them go].
And regardless of what else you put on, wear love [loving your friend from the center of who you are, never faking it].

—Colossians 3:12-14 (*The Message*)

Remember and practice that, and friendship is really going to look good on you, girl!

You're Good to Go

Bet you saw this coming ... Get together with your friend or group and get to work on those Friendship Flubs.

What you'll need:

+ this book
+ paper and pens (the fun kind, of course!)
+ honesty
+ imagination

What to do:

Decide which Friendship Flub you want to work on together. For example, if you're the only one with a jealousy challenge, but you both (or all) struggle with gossiping, pick The Rumor Tumor or Worthless Words.

Now answer these questions together and write down your answers (you'll only need one copy):

★ When was the last time it happened?
★ What exactly took place?
★ Why did it happen?
★ What was the worst thing about it?

Okay, here's the fun part. Come up with a special signal you will give each other the next time that Friendship Flub starts to happen. You could pull on your left earlobe if drama begins. Cough when an opportunity for gossip arises. Do a big stretch (arms over head) when jealousy starts to rear its ugly little head.

Then wait for it! Decide on a reward you can give yourselves when you avoid that flub for a whole week. Could you pool your allowance and go for ice cream? Watch *Flicka* together for the

forty-fifth time? Make it something you will all look forward to —
and dive into it with all the fun you can have. You deserve it!

That's What I'm Talkin' About!

In the days ahead, write, draw, or doodle your responses to
what happens with your friends.

We ALMOST flubbed (or did) when _____

_____

_____

_____

The signal really worked when _____

_____

_____

_____

Fixing our flub is harder (or easier) than I thought it would
be because _____

_____

_____

_____

chapter four

Not a Friend
IN SIGHT

F orget about her, Em," Mary Elizabeth said.

Kimberly bobbed her head until Emily was sure it would topple off. "We don't need her if she's going to act like this."

"But this is so not Lara!" Emily wailed.

She sank into the bus seat and looked glumly out the window, and then down at her hands, and then up at the chewing gum-dotted ceiling. Anywhere but at Lara, who was in front with the Price Tags, whispering behind her hand and glancing over her shoulder and rolling her eyes as if she were Katy Cuthbert's clone. It just hurt too much to see it.

Next to her, Mary Elizabeth folded her arms across her chest, the way Emily's mother did when she meant business.

"Kimberly and I are there for you, Em," she said. "But you're gonna have to just forget about her and move on."

Kimberly nodded again. "Don't go running after her like a little puppy dog."

"I just want Lara back." Emily's eyes blurred, and she pressed her fingers into them so the whole bus wouldn't see her blubbering in the back seat. She heard Mary Elizabeth sigh.

"Okay, like I said, we're here for you. Just let us know when you're ready to get over it, and we'll have some real fun."

"Right," Kimberly said. "Who needs Lara Lillo anyway?"

I do, Emily wanted to tell them. Instead, she slumped into the corner and imagined the scary things she'd been running away from all day: No Lara sharing peanut butter crackers and giggles at lunch and recess. No Lara to call when she was freaked out or jazzed or just plain bored. Getting through hurt feelings and evil boys and first bras without Lara. Never again giggling so hard they almost went unconscious. Or talking silently across the Sunday school room. Or standing up for each other — to the Price Tag Girls.

Emily couldn't hold it back any longer. She sobbed until it was time for her to get off the bus. She was sure Lara and her new friends didn't notice, because now she was in a world all by herself.

That Is SO Me

Most girls experience that friendless feeling at some time, and it's worse than having a cavity filled or cleaning the toilets. This "self survey" is a chance for you to let go and explore that feeling. Work with it even if you're perfectly happy with your friends right now. You never know what you might find out.

Read what's in each of the four boxes. Put a star next to the one that best describes you most of the time.

Friendless in Girl World

Maybe you've just moved to a new school or a different class. Or your old friends have made new ones. Or you just haven't been able to find close buds to be with. Whatever the reason, you feel alone and empty and even scared. Maybe it's even hard to go to school, where all the "friend slots" have been filled, and you don't seem to fit in anywhere.

Friend-Challenged

You have friends, but you don't get along a lot of the time. Or maybe you don't like the way they treat you or each other or people outside the group. Could be you'd like to find other friends who are kinder or who are interested in having an actual happy friendship — but you haven't found any. In fact, you're not sure you even know where to start.

Two or Three Is Company

You have one BFF, or maybe three of you girls hang out together. You're content with your little tribe, and you're not out there looking for new buds to add. Maybe sometimes you wonder what it would be like to have more girls in your circle of friends. Perhaps you even get lonely when your BFF isn't available. But most of the time, being two or three is just right.

Miss Congeniality

There's your BFF, and a maybe few other girls who are right up there with her, and then perhaps you have a bunch of friends you love for a lot of different reasons. In fact, you can barely walk down the hall at school without saying hi to at least three people you could hang out with, no problem. Maybe it's a little crowded in your life sometimes — like when you can only have twelve girls for a sleepover and you can't decide which dozen of your close friends to invite. But mostly, you wouldn't trade your friend-filled life with anyone's.

If you starred "*Friendless in Girl World*," don't give up hope. There are friends out there for everyone, and this chapter will help you discover them and show them that their lives will be so much fuller if they have you for a pal. Look forward to it!

If you starred "*Friend-Challenged*," there's no reason to stay stuck with girls who don't make good friends. Friendship is supposed to be fun and happy and loving. This chapter can help you end unhappy relationships if you need to and lead you to the kind you're longing for. Who knows, it could even be with girls who are also "Friend-Challenged," or even "Friendless in Girl World." How cool is that?

If you starred "*Two or Three Is Company*," get a big ol' smile on your face because you are blessed. But don't miss out on the possibility of getting to know new people too — including girls who are "Friendless" or "Friend-Challenged" — even if they don't become new close friends (though maybe they will!). This chapter will help you check out those opportunities and have even more good stuff to share with the sister friends you have now.

If you starred "*Miss Congeniality*," keep reading. This chapter will help you be sure at least one of your many friends lets you be bummed when you're bummed and doesn't expect you to be the world's cheerleader 24/7. This chapter can also lead you in ways to make those who are "Friendless in Girl World," and currently "Friend-Challenged" feel less alone. If anyone can do it, you can.

One thing is for sure: God wants us to have friends. He has provided people with good buds since the world began:

* ❉ Abraham and his nephew Lot
* ❉ Ruth and Naomi
* ❉ David and Jonathon
* ❉ Job and his buddies (Even though they didn't give Job such great advice, at least they were there for him.)
* ❉ Mary and Elizabeth enjoyed being pregnant together.
* ❉ Jesus' twelve disciples were as close to each other as brothers (even though they argued like brothers too).
* ❉ And Paul talked about his friends — Peter, Silas, and Timothy, to name only a few — in every letter he wrote in the New Testament.

The need for people to travel with through a Christ-following life — or even just elementary or middle school! — hasn't changed. Jesus said,

> "For where two or three come together in my name, there am I with them."
>
> —Matthew 18:20

So let's find out how to draw right into your life the best friends for you.

Here's the Deal

Here are some tips for being a friend magnet if you're new or totally friendless:

Accept that it's normal to be nervous when you try to make new friends. Even the girl who was voted Most Popular in her old school will wonder as she faces a classroom full of strangers, "Will they dis me? What if nobody likes me? What if I never make another friend my whole life?" Don't wait for those butterflies-on-steroids in your stomach to go away. Just take a deep breath and go on to the next step.

Start slowly. Just as you're checking people out for possible friendships, they're looking for what you're all about too. The best things in life take time, including BFF-ships.

Begin by smiling and saying hi to kids who seem friendly and people you'd like to get to know. Don't wait for them to come to you with, "Hi, wanna be best friends?" You don't have to tackle them, either. Just let it show that you're open to meeting new people.

Then start conversations.

* Ask the girl who sits behind you where she got such a cool backpack.
* Comment on the cute puppy picture the girl next to you has on her binder.
* Compliment that girl on the bus for sticking up for her little sister.
* Ask a girl you'd like to befriend to help you with something. People like to share what they know with somebody who cares. It will give you a chance to get to know her in the process. A complete klutz in PE? Ask that girl who shoots baskets like she's in the WNBA if she'll work with you on your layups. Having trouble learning the names of the people in your class? See if that girl who obviously knows everybody will tutor you on who's who.
* Listen more than you talk. (You have two ears and only one mouth, so what does that tell you?) Ask questions and really pay attention to what that possible new friend says. If she sees that you're actually interested in what she

thinks, she'll probably want to be your bud. Good listeners are hard to find!

* Be as close to the real you as you can while you're doing all this. If you pretend to be a certain way just to have someone to eat lunch with, you're in for friendship indigestion! Show the true you, because people dig girls who are genuinely themselves.

Do you want new friends because your old ones aren't good for you?

First, make sure it's time for a break off and not just a case of a friendship flub that can actually be fixed. You definitely need to part ways with a toxic friend — one who often leaves you feeling bad about yourself and bummed out about your friendship. But if there's still a lot of good in your relationship, see if the suggestions in chapter 3 can help you keep it together.

If you've tried to solve the problems and it isn't working, tell your friend or group good-bye with a polite, honest, calm explanation. Something like this:

"Look, the way you treat me (or each other, or other people) just doesn't work for me. I've tried to talk to you about it, but nothing's changed, so I think we should take a break from each other. I don't hate you. I just think this is the right thing to do."

Give yourself time and space to be sad. No matter how bad things have gotten, at one time you had hopes for your friendship, and it's hard to watch them go away. Talk to your parents or someone else you trust. Don't put down your ex-friends — just talk about how *you* feel.

Then make a fresh start by doing things like

* sitting in a different seat on the bus;
* asking your teacher if you can move to another desk (if you sit next to your former friend in class);

* joining other girls at lunch, and talking about anything but your recent breakup; and
* taking the steps for making new friends on pages 75–77.

This time, don't settle for anything less than a friend who doesn't pull you down or hold you back; who loves you because you're you; and who helps you be your true, fabulous self, just as you do for her. No friend will be flawless, so just look for one (or more) whose flaws you can smile at.

If you break off a toxic friendship, don't be surprised if your ex-friend asks (or begs) you to change your mind. Give her another chance if you think there's hope for working things out, but stay true to what you know makes a good friendship. On the other hand, she might also turn on you because she's hurt, maybe by talking trash about you or trying to keep other girls from being your friend. Let that pass if you can and go on with your quest for good friends. If things really get out of hand, go to her and ask her, kindly, to stop. If she doesn't, read in chapter 5 about how to handle girls who turn mean. Whatever you do, don't get pulled into her drama.

You may find yourself at some point in a group of friends that gets along great, except for that one girl who makes everyone crazy. Maybe she tries too hard to be funny. Or she's turned into a boy chaser. Or she's making herself the boss of everyone. Maybe she uses you girls when she needs something or spreads all the group's secrets to the entire school, complete with exaggerations. Do you do a group ditch? Actually, you may have to break off your relationship with her as a group if she doesn't respond to the fix-its in Chapter 3, but do it as kindly as you would just one friend. Definitely don't be mean to her or dis her to other people. If she's hurting your circle of friends, distance yourselves from her in love. But first, work with her, help her, and be honest with her.

Here's how you can add friends to your life:

+ Make sure your present friends know you aren't ditching them. Reassure them that your wanting to get to know more people doesn't mean they aren't the best friends on the planet already.
+ Don't force anything. Look at the steps on pages 75–77 [friend magnet] and take them gently.

+ Think about things you'd like to do that you haven't tried because your friends aren't interested. Then give one of those things a try.
+ Go to an after-school activity you haven't tried before, like a Bible study or Girl Scouts or the drama club.
+ Take lessons in swimming or some other sport. Maybe you could be on the community team.
+ Learn to Rollerblade or take up sign language or brush up on your acting skills — anything that you'd love to do that will also give you a chance to meet new people who love those things too.
+ Be on the lookout for girls who seem lonely. You never know what you might have in common that could be the beginning of a surprising new friendship.

If you're surrounded by friends, spread that sparkle:

* Be the one who welcomes the new girl and introduces her to everyone you know — since you know everybody!
* Ask the girl who doesn't seem to have good friends what she likes to do. As the "social director," you can probably help her find someone to play chess with or who shares her love for *Anne of Green Gables* or a could-be pal who also digs the trampoline.
* Encourage the girl who just split with a friend. Be someone she can talk to when she's feeling low. Tell her what you like about her. You may not become her new BFF (you already have six!), but you can give her support in a time of change.

Make sure that while you're helping everyone else, you have someone you can whine to, cry with, and depend on for cheering up when *you* need it. Friendships — no matter how many you have — should always work both ways.

There's almost nothing more painful than being
rejected, especially by someone you thought was going to be
your friend literally forever. But it happens all the time — often like
this:

* A BFF starts making excuses not to do things with you.
* She suddenly won't IM you back and she's always "busy"
  when you call her.
* She or someone else tells you she doesn't want to be your
  friend anymore.
* She hangs out with another girl and acts like *she's* her best
  friend.
* She stops talking to you and ignores you, especially when
  the new friend is around.

It's even worse if her new friend is someone you've both been
friends with, who seems to have totally stolen your BFF from you.

And what's mega-worse is when a whole group of friends
dumps you, all at once. That's not just painful — it's agony.

All of the suggestions in this chapter for making new friends
can work for you. But first give yourself a chance to recover from
an experience that makes you feel sick inside.

Try talking to the friend who ditched you (though you can
just move on if you think that's best). Be calm and honest and
simply ask her what went wrong. If there is actually something
you've done that made her think you weren't a good friend, see if
she's willing to work on it with you. If so, do the best you can to
help your friendship without losing the real you. Chapter 3 can
help.

If there's no fixing it, walk away calmly without creating any
drama. Hold your tears, pillow-punching, and venting for when
you get home with your mom, big sis, or some other understanding

person (but probably not another girl your age). Take some alone time for that if it helps you.

Talk to God about it, either with your voice or in a journal. God can take all the venom you want to spew. Tell it all to God, just like the writers of the psalms did. Check out Psalm 109 for inspiration!

Then remind yourself that you are a God-made, God-loved person who is worthy of a friend who cherishes your friendship.

Go back to your activities with your head held high and, as you're ready, follow the steps on pages 75–77 (friend magnet steps).

Don't give up or avoid things you enjoy because your former friend is there. It might hurt to see her with a new BFF, but you have a right to do the things you love. Your courage will attract new friends, and you'll feel better about you.

You're Good to Go

Making a "Friend Gallery" is the perfect thing to do right here. You can do it with your BFF or group or create it on your own if you don't have close friends right now, but you have had in the past. If you've just never found good buds, create your gallery with people you would like to be friends with, even if at this point they're only in your imagination.

What you'll need:

- ✄ photographs or drawings of ALL your friends — even those you don't see often (or you can use pictures from magazines that remind you of each of them)
- ✄ a piece of heavy paper or posterboard, any size you want as long as it's big enough for all your pictures

✁ glue or paste

✁ fun pens or markers

✁ a big enough space for you and your BFF or friend group
to work

What to do:

Paste the pictures to the paper as if they were arranged on a
wall in an art gallery (or the way your mom or dad displays the
family photos). Leave space to write under each one. Draw or
glue fun frames around each one.

Under each picture, write what you like about that friend. You
can include what you have in common, how she makes your life
better, and what special thing she brings to the friendship.

What it tells you:

◆ That you probably have more friends than you thought,
even if all of them aren't BFFs or in your life daily.

◆ That each person is your friend for a different reason.

◆ That maybe there are empty places in your life where it
would be good to have new friends. (Do you need someone who likes art the way you do? Someone who gets
what it's like to have divorced parents? Somebody you
can laugh with because you are always helping your cur-
rent friends with their problems?) That doesn't mean
you should drop the friends you have now. It just shows
there's room for more.

If you have trouble thinking of why you like a particular friend
because, frankly, she's not that nice to you, talk it over with a
grown-up you trust. Read pages 75–77. (friend magnet section) in
this chapter. You'll know what to do.

If you are making your friend gallery with friends, you'll all see at the same time that it's not only okay, it's good for people to have more friends than just each other. No single friend, or even one small circle of friends, can be everything to you — just as you can't be everything everyone wants you to be.

What to do now:

Do something to tell or show each of the friends in your gallery why she's important to you. Send emails. Make cards. Or just sit down and say it to her.

If you've realized you have a friend gap, or the friendships you have now aren't good for you, read through this chapter again and take one step to change that. Even a baby step will move you forward.

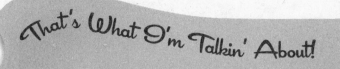
That's What I'm Talkin' About!

Write, draw, or doodle about what's happened since you made your Friends Gallery.

I feel more (or less) _____

_____

_____

_____

I've taken _____ steps to make new friends or to help other people find good buds. _____

_____

_____

I think I might like to make friends with _____ because she _____

_____

_____

_____

_____

chapter five

RMGs
(REALLY MEAN GIRLS)

When Katy and the Price Tag Girls made their entrance into the classroom, Emily sat up straight in her desk, pretending to be fascinated with a library book on the Declaration of Independence. Out of the corner of her eye, Emily saw that Lara was with them. After three days of practically worshiping Katy and completely ignoring Emily, it was obvious she was a P.T. Girl now.

Emily felt the now-familiar hot tears in her eyes threatening to make a scene, but she chewed on her lower lip and watched the picture of Thomas Jefferson blur before her. Her mom had told her she was sure Lara would realize she'd made a mistake and leave the clique soon. She said for Emily to keep her chin up and not let this bring her down.

That was easy for her mom to say. Emily hadn't told her all that was happening every day. It would have been bad enough if Lara had just dumped her as a BFF, but —

"Hey, Emily Ellen."

Emily froze. The only person who was allowed to call her that, the one person in school who even *knew* her middle name, was Lara.

But it was Katy talking.

She stood over Emily, tapping her manicured nails on Emily's desktop.

"Don't you know it's rude not to look at somebody when they're talking to you?" Katy said.

As hard as she stiffened her neck so she wouldn't, Emily looked up at her. Katy's lip was curled like she was sniffing someone's armpit.

"What?" Emily said.

"Lara wants to know — only she won't ask you herself for *obvious* reasons — if you still have her sunglasses in your backpack. You know, the cute green ones."

Emily glanced past Katy at Lara, who was staring into the face of one of the other Tags and trying not to laugh. Emily knew that expression, just like she knew what everything meant that ever crossed Lara's face.

"So ... do you still have them?" Katy's voice was sharp, like Emily's mom when she was fed up with the kids at home.

"Yes, I have them," Emily said stiffly.

"Are they still in one piece? Lara says you break things sometimes when you get all mad."

"I do not!"

"Are you saying she's a liar?"

"No!"

Katy smiled. At least, Emily thought that was what she was trying to do. She had on her Mr. Potato Head lips again.

"Well, anyway," she said, "it doesn't matter. Lara wants you to keep them."

A tiny spark of hope flickered up in Emily's heart. Lara wasn't cutting her off completely. She wanted Emily to have the sunglasses she'd gotten when they were at the beach together ...

"Yeah," Katy went on, "she says your face is so fat you've probably stretched them out by now, so she wouldn't be able to keep them on anyway."

Emily felt her skin go hot, and she couldn't keep her chin from dropping. It was apparently just the reaction the Price Tags were hoping for, because they split open into laughter as if they could no longer hold it in. Emily didn't look to see if Lara was laughing with them. She didn't want to know.

The bell rang, and Katy returned to her followers. Emily felt so sick she actually gagged.

Five minutes later she was in the nurse's office hoping she wouldn't throw up. She spent the whole period with a cold washcloth on her forehead, trying to figure out what to do. *Keep your chin up,* Mom had said. *Do whatever you usually do.*

Okay. When the bell rang, she put on a smile that felt as plastic as Katy's and went back to her class for the science experiment. Everyone was paired up except Emily and the new girl, Tia. She didn't look happy about working with Emily.

What was the deal? She didn't even *know* Emily.

"You don't have to worry," Emily told her. "I usually do pretty good in science."

Tia nodded wisely. "Yeah, I heard you like to brag about yourself."

"Who told you that?" Emily said, and then she put up her hand. "I know. Katy."

"No," Tia said. "It was that nice girl, Lara."

Emily couldn't answer. Her throat was too tight for words.

And by lunchtime, she was sure she'd choke to death. Before she could even get through the cafeteria line — not that she felt like eating — she heard everything from *"Emily Ellen — what a lame name"* to "You really DO have fat cheeks" to "You think you're all that — and you're SO not!" Most of it was from people she didn't really even know.

At least she had Mary Elizabeth and Kimberly to eat with. But when she got to their table, they looked at each other as if a black widow spider had just joined them.

"What?" Emily said.

Kimberly poked Mary Elizabeth, who said, in a hurt voice, "Why did you say all that stuff about us, Emily?"

"What stuff?"

"You said I was Miss Chatty-Chat-Chat and couldn't keep a secret."

Kimberly, as usual, nodded. "And you told everybody about my birthmark. And we all promised never to tell that to anybody else!"

"I didn't! Honest!" The words barely squeaked out. Emily switched to shaking her head, hard.

"What you did to Lara was the worst, though," Mary Elizabeth said. "No wonder she went over to the Price Tags."

"I didn't do anything to her!" Emily managed to say.

But neither Mary Elizabeth nor Kimberly was looking at Emily anymore. Their gazes lifted to a figure at the end of the table. It was Lara.

Emily couldn't get any words to come out. It didn't matter. Lara had obviously come to talk to Mary Elizabeth and Kimberly. She grabbed Kimberly's hand and nodded to Mary Elizabeth, and without a glance back at Emily, the three of them moved like one six-legged bug, over to Katy's table.

"Loser," somebody said as he passed by.

Now even the boys were in on it. Emily pushed her lunch away and left the cafeteria. Her chin was nearly buried in her chest.

That Is SO Me

Nasty, huh? Emily is suffering from one of the worst plagues in girlhood: girl bullying. You probably recognize it because you've seen it done, you've had it pulled on you, or you've bullied someone yourself. Take a look at your own experience with Really Mean Girls just to get the big picture of bullying in your mind. No matter what your results are, this chapter can help, so be honest.

As you read each behavior under "Have You Ever" on the left side, put a star in the column that's true for you. You might have more than one star (*) in each row, and you may have none in some rows.

Have You Ever ...	I've Done It Often	I've Had It Done to Me Often by Certain Girls	I've Seen It Done by Certain Girls
decided who's in and who's out?		*	
suddenly excluded a girl from parties?			*
suddenly excluded a girl from conversations?	*	*	
completely ignored a former friend as if she's invisible?	*		
spread rumors about a particular girl?		*	
gossiped about a girl at every opportunity?		*	
rolled eyes in disgust right at a girl?			*

	I've Done It Often	I've Had It Done to Me Often by Certain Girls	I've Seen It Done by Certain Girls
whispered about a girl in her presence so she'd know she was being talked about?	☒	☒	☐
pointed at a girl in a rude way?	☐	☒	☐
taunted a girl (not friendly teasing)?	☐	☐	☒
sneered at a girl?	☐	☐	☐
laughed unkindly to a girl's face?	☐	☐	☐
threatened to exclude a girl if she wouldn't meet demands?	☐	☐	☐
threatened a girl with physical harm?	☐	☐	☐
deliberately accused a girl of something she didn't do?	☐	☐	☐
used phone calls or the Internet to intimidate a girl?	☐	☐	☐
asked other girls to shun someone?	☐	☐	☒
passed nasty notes about a girl?	☐	☐	☒
given a girl threatening looks or made threatening gestures at her?	☐	☐	☐

	I've Done It Often	I've Had It Done to Me Often by Certain Girls	I've Seen It Done by Certain Girls
been nice to a girl in private but mean to her in public?	☐	✖	✖
ruined a girl's other friendships?	✖ *~~twice~~ once*	✖	☐
hurt a girl physically and on purpose?	☐	☐	☐
damaged a girl's belongings on purpose?	☐	☐	✖
laughed at inside jokes in front of a girl who wasn't in on them?	☐	☐	☐
given a girl an ugly code name?	☐	☐	✖
written ugly graffiti about a girl?	☐	☐	☐
given the silent treatment when a girl asks, "Are you mad at me?"	✖	☐	☐
acted nice to a girl to her face and destroyed her behind her back?	☐	☐	☐
"graded" girls on how cool they are (or aren't)?	✖	✖	☐
built an alliance against a particular girl?	☐	☐	☐

*9 mid
7 rights
6 Lefts*

I've Done It Often

If you have any stars in this column, you have been—and maybe still are—guilty of bullying. That doesn't mean you're a heinous person. It does mean you *have to* stop those kinds of behaviors and learn ways to feel good about your life that don't hurt other people. It can be hard to see what you're doing and even harder to stop, but you can do it. This chapter can help. There's a God-made, God-loved person in you that doesn't want to do this stuff.

If you have any stars at all in this column, you have been the victim of bullying and maybe still are. It is NOT okay for people to treat you that way. You have done nothing to deserve it, no matter how many friendship flubs you may have committed. Hang in there, because this chapter will help you deal with bullies and feel like the strong, confident, loveable girl you truly are.

I've Had It Done to Me Often by Certain Girls

If you have any stars at all in this column, you've seen bullying happen. No matter how you reacted to it, if you haven't done anything to stop it, this chapter is for you too. It will help you recognize Really Mean Girls and decide they can't be allowed to keep hurting people. Chapter Six will give you ways to take action (that don't turn YOU into a bully).

I've Seen It Done by Certain Girls

See if you recognize this typical Really Mean Girl, who takes part in any or all of the actions described in "That Is SO Me."

She knows what she's doing and does it on purpose; these are not accidental friendship flubs. This is deliberate and it happens continually (not just once in a while).

She does things just to make other people feel less than she is; she has to be on top at all times.

She shows open dislike for people she thinks are beneath her (not as cool as she is, or as smart, or as well-dressed ... you get the idea).

She continues her bullying, creating a threat that doesn't go away and probably gets worse.

She can't stand people who are "different" (race, physical challenge, learning disability, or even just being from another part of the country).

She tries to get other people to shun her Target, leaving the bullied girl isolated and alone.

She can act like she cares but only uses that to get what she wants.

She usually has a group of "friends" working with her (or for her!).

She does her dirty work when adults aren't around; teachers often think she's perfectly lovely.

She refuses to accept responsibility when she hurts people; she never feels sorry and certainly never says she is.

Although anybody can qualify for this Bully Princess's cruel treatment, her usual target is a girl who

* has some annoying behaviors (loud laugh, chews with her mouth open) OR
* is new to the class or the school (which makes her "different") OR

* is very sensitive (which means she'll give the bully exactly the emotional reaction she's looking for) OR
* doesn't have a whole lot of self-confidence yet (so she's easily convinced she's everything the bully says she is) OR
* stands out because of her race or religion or a physical challenge (which gives the bully plenty of good material for taunting and mean gossip) OR
* isn't easily intimidated because she's independent and speaks her mind (so the bully is challenged to take her down) OR
* is unique because she's smart, gifted, or talented (which means the bully has to make her look inferior so she can be the one at the top) OR
* just doesn't fit what the bully sees as normal. Maybe she plays with dolls, reads books constantly, has a big vocabulary, or doesn't care about clothes, boys, and gossip. This girl doesn't realize that, of course, the RMG thinks she can decide what everyone should do.

The dangerous thing about RMGs is that they know they can create something like a hamster wheel for their targets, so their bullying can go on and on and the victim will feel worse and worse. It goes something like this:

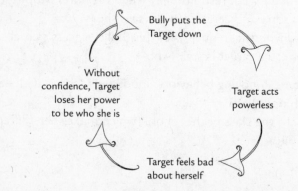

Bully puts the Target down

Target acts powerless

Target feels bad about herself

Without confidence, Target loses her power to be who she is

Each time this occurs, the Target loses more of her power to simply be who she truly is. That makes her easier and easier to bully, until she feels hopeless. This is NOT just part of growing up. It should NEVER happen. It causes feelings that don't just go away when the girl grows up. (Just ask your mom if she remembers any girl bullies when she was your age, and then watch the sparks — or the tears — come to her eyes.) A girl who's bullied may do one or more of these things:

* She becomes convinced that she's everything the bully says she is; her personality actually changes as she believes she's a loser. How sad is that?
* She gets depressed and starts doing poorly in school or makes up excuses not to go. Depression can be a frightening thing.
* She becomes physically ill with headaches or stomach problems that can continue even when she's a grown-up.
* She tries to get back at the bullies and becomes one herself. That twists her personality too.
* She eventually thinks that nobody can be trusted (especially if the bully is a former friend) and from then on hesitates to believe in real friendship.

And yet, a girl who's bullied may not tell anyone — like a mom or a teacher or a counselor — because

✖ she doesn't realize it's bullying; she just thinks it's girl stuff she should be able to handle.

✖ she's ashamed that she's being bullied or that she can't do anything to stop it.

✖ she's afraid the bully will do something worse to get back at her for telling.

✖ she doesn't think anybody can really help.

✖ she doesn't think anybody WILL help because grown-ups really like this bully girl (they've never seen her in action).

✖ she doesn't want to be branded as a "tattletale."

At its worst, bullying can cause physical harm:

Some girls come to feel so bad about themselves, they think they deserve to be hurt, and they cut themselves on purpose.

Violence — yes, actual beating people up — breaks out in places like school buses, athletic fields, and girls' restrooms. On one website, you can see 2,000 videos of real girls fighting! How absolutely gross is that? Sometimes the bully starts it. Sometimes the girl being bullied gets fed up and starts punching. It happens in every kind of neighborhood and school.

A number of girls in elementary and middle school have tried to take their own lives because they couldn't stand the bullying any longer and thought it would never end. Some of those girls have succeeded.

It doesn't have to be that way! You CAN stop bullying from happening to you. Let's start, as always, with God.

The Bible has so much to say about bullying, it won't all fit here, so you'll find more advice from God in the next section too. The verses here will help you see that God is there to help the Target. He always has been.

In Psalm 55, the psalm writer has obviously been bullied:

I shudder at the mean voice, quail before the evil eye,
As they pile on the guilt, stockpile angry slander.

—Psalm 55:3 (*The Message*)

And not by random mean girls:
This isn't the neighborhood bully mocking me—I could take that ...
It's you! We grew up together!
You! My best friend!

Those long hours of leisure as we walked arm in arm, God a third party to our conversation.

—Psalm 55:12-14 (*The Message*)

Ouch! That *really* hurts. But the psalmist goes straight to God:

I call to God;
GOD will help me.
At dusk, dawn, and noon I sigh deep sighs—he hears, he rescues.
My life is well and whole, secure in the middle of danger
Even while thousands are lined up against me.
God hears it all and ... puts them in their place.

—Psalm 55:16-19 (*The Message*)

He isn't finished venting. This is painful stuff that won't go away easily:

And this, my best friend, betrayed his [or her] best friends; his life betrayed his word.
All my life I've been charmed by his speech, never dreaming he'd turn on me.
His words, which were music to my ears, turned to daggers in my heart.

—Psalm 55:20-21 (*The Message*)

But things work out for him and he has encouraging words for you:

Pile your troubles on
GOD's shoulders—he'll
carry your load, he'll
help you out....
[God] I trust in you.

—Psalm 55:22-23
(*The Message*)

It's true. Even if you feel you can't tell anybody else about the bullying, go to God and pour it all out. Write to God in a journal. Get it out in a poem to God. Or just talk, out loud, into your pillow or at your favorite teddy bear. (Psalm 140 gives you a model for how to do that.) Then be still. Get yourself calm. You may not hear God's actual voice (that's very rare), but without even realizing it, you will be filled with God's love and protection. That will give you the strength to take your next steps to stop the bullying.

If you want to read more in the Bible about God helping with bullying, go to Psalm 17; 34:17 – 18; 38:11 – 16; 41; 56; 62; and 112:7. You will be pumped up to do the right thing about bullies.

All you need to remember is that God will never let you down; he'll never let you be pushed past your limit; he'll always be there to help you come through it.

– 1 Corinthians 10:13
(*The Message*)

If you think about it, Jesus was bullied worse than just about anybody in history. In one single scene, a group of soldiers delivered every kind of peer abuse possible:

The soldiers assigned to the governor took Jesus into the governor's palace and got the entire brigade together for some fun. They stripped him and dressed him in a red toga. They plaited a crown from branches of a thornbush and set it on his head. They put a stick in his right hand for a scepter. Then they knelt before him in mocking reverence: "Bravo, King of the Jews!" they said. "Bravo!" Then they spit on him and hit him on the head with the stick.

–Matthew 27:27-30
(*The Message*)

"The right words will be there; the Spirit of your Father will supply the words."

–Matthew 10:19-20
(*The Message*)

Throughout his time on earth (not just when he was about to be crucified), Jesus set an example for how to act if we have bullies in our lives, because he definitely dealt with mean people. He said that bullying is definitely wrong, but when you're bullied, you have a chance to show how a real follower of Christ behaves. So try not to worry.

Here's the Deal

Now, let's get your mind straight about how to handle bullies.

If a bully tries to scare you into thinking you're nothing or nobody, remember that there's nothing she can do to take away who you are. She doesn't even *know* who you are (obviously!), so your power to be you is safe. Believe in that so you won't run away crying. Running away gives the bully a reason to pick on you some more.

> "There's nothing they can do to your soul, your core being. Save your fear [awe] for God, who holds your entire life – body and soul – in his hands."
>
> –Matthew 10:28 (*The Message*)

With your real friends you can be honest about your feelings, talk things over, and work out your problems. *You cannot do that with a bully*. Bullying isn't about friendship. It's about power. You can't deal with a bully the way you do a friend. The *worst* thing you can do is tell or show her that she's hurting you. That's what she *wants* to do! Give her what she wants, and she'll keep on. Take it away, and she's got nothin'.

Here's how to do that:

If a girl or her group just shuts you out (which is very painful), "'quietly withdraw. Don't make a scene. Shrug your shoulders and be on your way'" (Matthew 10:14, *The Message*). Do you really want to be friends with people who treat you that way? You DO need to feel like you belong. You DON'T need to be in a closed clique. Not to worry. You won't be without true friends for long. (See chapter 4.)

Whatever a bully does to you—whether she excludes you, insults you, gossips about you, threatens you, or does you bodily harm—pretend it doesn't matter until you can get to a safe place. Of course, it DOES matter, but you can't let her see that. When Jesus was taken before Pilate, and everybody was saying horrible stuff about him, Jesus didn't give them the satisfaction of a reply. "But Jesus made no reply, not even to a single charge—to the great amazement of the governor" (Matthew 27:14).

You do have that choice. Frankly, anything else is like punching your fist into a brick wall.

Don't avoid the bully unless you're in physical danger. Go where you always go. Sit where you usually sit. Do what you're in the habit of doing. Do not let her think she can cut you off from your own life. It may be hard to go to your locker when she and her cronies are waiting to grab your backpack and empty it into the trash can. The steps below will help you with that. Inside, keep saying, "I am free. I live my life the way I know is right. Nobody can stop me." That is the truth. What she does and says is not. If you're really concerned, ask some other girls to go with you, but don't become a bully gang of your own. Everyone in the group should ignore the bully and focus on keeping you safe.

Do *not* fight back. Don't try to give her what she's dishing out to you, because you're better than that. Don't try to show her who's boss. This is what is meant by "turn the other cheek."

"Do not resist an evil person. If someone strikes you on the right cheek, turn to him [or her] the other also."

—Matthew 5:39

Jesus wasn't saying to go ahead and let people beat up on you. He was telling you not to join them in their miserable game. Here's what that looks like:

Bully: Don't you have any mirrors in your house?

You **(DON'T SAY)**: Yeah, want to borrow one so you can look at your ugly face?

You **(DO SAY)**: You know what? I think you just feel like you need to be mean to somebody today, but I'm not your girl. (Then go on about your business, ignoring anything else she might want to add.)

Bully (to another girl, but loud enough to be heard by you): There's that little liar.

You **(DON'T SAY)**: I know you're talking about me. Well, it takes one to know one!

You **(DO SAY)**: I heard you, but I'm not listening (or just ignore her with a smile).

Bully: I don't know why you even come to school. Nobody likes you.

You **(DON'T SAY)**: Why do you have to be so mean? I hate you! OR You could have fooled me. I have a lot of friends. OR Who peed in your breakfast cereal this morning? (As good as it might feel to come out with that!)

You **(DO SAY)**: *You* obviously don't like me. Too bad we can't be friends, then.

Bully: No offense, but your breath, like, totally stinks. Ewww! Don't come in the lunchroom, you'll make everybody sick.

You **(DON'T SAY)**: Oh, you noticed my camel breath? Nothing gets by you, does it?

You **(DO SAY)**: I'm not going there with you. We're both better than that. (What is she going to say? "No, I am NOT better than that!"?)

Bully: If you ask her to sit at our table, you are out of the group.

You **(DON'T SAY)**: Okay, okay—just please don't dump me.

You **(DO SAY)**: Are you kidding me? You really think you can get to me with that?

What you are doing when you give those don't-fight-back answers is **taking back the power to be yourself**. You are a child of God, God's own kid. You're trying to be like Jesus, not like the bully.

Keep in mind that you are probably not going to change the bully. That isn't your mission right now. Your job is to let God heal your heart, so you don't turn into her, and so that you become a strong example for other people for how to live a Jesus life. What you do may make a huge difference in you in the best way possible—from the inside out. That way no Bully Princess—

Go ahead and be angry. You do well to be angry—but don't use your anger as fuel for revenge. And don't stay angry. Don't go to bed angry. Don't give the Devil that kind of foothold in your life.

—Ephesians 4:26-27
(*The Message*)

If what a bully says about you has a little bit of truth in it, that really hurts. Just remember that it's the way she says it that is mean and not okay. When you're ready, you can consider whether you could be cleaner and neater when you come to school, or if you might actually stop trying so hard to be funny and just be yourself. But do those things because they will make you more genuine, not because you want to avoid being bullied.

or anyone else who pressures you—can determine what you do and say and how you live.

Jesus asks us to go one step further than that.

"You're familiar with the old written law, 'Love your friend,' and its unwritten companion, 'Hate your enemy.' I'm challenging that. I'm telling you to love your enemies. Let them bring out the best in you, not the worst. When someone gives you a hard time, respond with the energies of prayer, for then you are working out of your true selves, your God-created selves."

—Matthew 5:43-45 (*The Message*)

What? This RMG does all this dirty, rotten stuff to you, and you're supposed to love her? Yikes! Could Jesus make it just a little bit harder, maybe? Before you decide you cannot possibly do that, Jesus isn't saying to go hang out with her, try to be her friend, let her stomp all over you. Here's what he's telling you to do:

Pray for her. Not, "Father, please make her go cross-eyed and let a bushel of basketballs fall on her head." And not, "God, thank you that I'm a better person than she is." Simply pray that God will heal whatever is making her be such an RMG, because nobody is just born to bully.

Have compassion for her. That means feel bad for her because she isn't seeing what a great person you are. It may seem like she has it all, including power, but deep inside she's really unhappy with herself. Being mean never gives a person joy, so she's actually pretty miserable. Be soft toward her in your heart, even though you can't trust her with your feelings.

Avoid telling everyone what a mean little brat she's being. She may be doing that to you, but as a Christ-follower, you don't get to do that to her.

Forgive her. Again, that doesn't mean tell her it's okay that she has made school a torture chamber. It isn't okay. But don't hold hate for her inside you. That only makes you full of hate—hateful. Let go of thoughts of wanting to get back at her or needing to see her suffer. That stuff will go through your head, but allow it to pass right on out. Otherwise, she still has control over you. Forgiveness sets you free.

It won't be easy, but, then, nobody ever promised it would be.

Let your real friend or friends know what you're trying to do and ask for support. You can even enlist the aid of girls you don't know very well but who seem to be non-bulliers. If you follow the steps above, you won't become another

> When they call us names, we say, "God bless you." When they spread rumors about *us*, we put in a good word for them."
>
> – 1 Corinthians 4: 12 - 13
> (*The Message*)

bully clique. You'll just be supported, and the bully will recognize that. There is safety in numbers.

If you have trouble with any of these steps, find an understanding adult woman who can help you come up with a plan (based on the above) that you can even write down and carry

There are certain bullying situations when it is VERY important that you tell an adult you trust what's going on and how it's affecting you. TELL if (1) you are in physical danger; (2) the bullying is affecting your grades; (3) you are physically sick because of the way the RMG is treating you; or (4) you feel so sad and hopeless you don't want to go to school or participate in the things you usually enjoy. TELLING IS NOT TATTLING! When you tattle, your purpose is to get the other person in trouble. When you tell, you do it to get yourself or someone else OUT of trouble. If you're in trouble because of a bully, keep telling adults until somebody helps you. Don't settle for, "Oh, this is just the way girls are." Don't give up until someone listens to you. Don't worry that the bully is going to make it worse for you if you tell. Real help will protect you and everyone else she picks on.

with you. It's always good to have someone to talk to who isn't involved and who can see things clearly. (This should not be someone who says, "Oh, for heaven's sake, just ignore them and they'll go away.")

Here's the Deal

...About Bullies in Cyberspace

Cyber bullying is anything cruel or harmful that's sent by email, Website, blog, IM, chat room, computer bulletin board, or cell phone.

A girl gets an email — or even a ton of emails — putting her down or threatening her. She can't tell who's sending them.

A girl receives IMs from unknown senders full of bad language, insults, and statements meant to scare her.

Somebody spreads a rumor about her on MySpace or even a website. Hundreds, thousands, even millions of people can read it.

Every time a girl turns on her computer or gets a text message on her phone, she's terrified she'll see another hideous picture of herself somebody has doctored up on the computer or a bunch of quotes from people saying gross, untrue things about her.

All of the things that are true about in-person bullying apply to cyber bullying, but in many ways, RMGs operating on a computer or cell phone have even MORE power to hurt:

✖ Instead of just the class or everybody in the cafeteria watching the bullying, everybody on the World Wide Web can see it!
✖ The girl being cyber bullied often doesn't even know who's doing it.
✖ It can be extremely difficult to find out who the RMG is.

✖ The abuser might even be someone she least suspects, since you don't have to be big or the leader of a mean clique to cyber bully. The bully can hide behind her computer and say whatever she wants.

✖ It happens right in the cyber-bullied girl's own home, maybe even her bedroom — her safe place. It can feel as if there's no getting away from it. She might even wake up in the morning to a nasty text message!

✖ Being able to read and reread what someone has said can actually cut deeper than just hearing it once.

✖ It can happen without adults even knowing what's going on.

✖ Other girls are willing to join in and gang up because no one knows who they are.

It's really sad, because the Internet gives everyone a chance to be heard, and some people have decided to use that chance to criticize or make fun of others. What can you do to protect yourself from that? You could just turn off your computer, but then you're cut out of getting information for schoolwork or communicating with your friends. It isn't fair for you to have to give up your email because somebody's abusing it.

First of all, do what you can to avoid being bullied in cyberspace:

✳ Never give out personal information in chat rooms and on IM.

✳ Don't share passwords, even with your best friends.

✳ Don't give people you don't know your cell phone number, instant messaging name, or email address, because they can use those things, pretending to be you.

✳ Use a screen name that doesn't give out anything about your age, gender, or location.

✳ Have someone help you learn about your email program from the Help menu. You can find out how to create folders, email filters, and folder routing. This can help shield you from hateful emails.

If you're the victim of cyber bullying, here's what you can do:

* Don't reply to any kind of communication that is abusive or obscene. The first time it happens, ignore it or log off.
* If it happens again, take action. Your service provider (that would be like Yahoo or Hotmail) should have a number that you can call to report abusive messaging. Have your mom or dad call it. You can even forward nasty emails to your service provider.

If it doesn't stop, try to find out who's doing it. Using Outlook or Outlook Express, click the right mouse button over an email to reveal details about where and who the email came from. Then get your parents to contact the school or service provider about the sender of the email. Remember this is telling, not tattling.

If the situation becomes serious—you are afraid all the time, you're feeling bad about yourself, or you think somebody might actually carry out a threat—save and print everything that's said about you so that if your parents need to take action, they'll have evidence.

If the cyber bullying is happening on a website, find out who hosts the site and report it (with your parents' help).

If the bullying includes physical threats, have your parents tell the police as well.

CYBER BULLYING IS AGAINST THE LAW! DON'T PUT UP WITH IT!

Here's the Deal

... If You Are a Bully

If you have any stars in first column of "That Is SO Me" and you are reading this section, good for you! That means

> *Cyber bullying is cowardly. People who do it hide in the Internet, because they know what they're doing is wrong. Cyber bullies shrink like the cowards they are when they know someone is onto them. You are brave. You can snuff out their mean words.*

you're willing to face what you're doing and that you want to change the behavior that may be tearing someone's heart to pieces. Keep reading, because what you'll learn here is not meant to make you feel like the worst person on earth. *What you're doing* is bad news, but you yourself are not "bad." You can change your behavior so that the true, amazing self you've been covering up can shine through. You really have a responsibility to do this, because you can turn the power you've been using in the wrong way to something that can change the world for the better. You obviously know how to influence people, so why not do it for God?

What to do:

Accept the fact that you have no right to insult, intimidate, threaten, or abuse another human being. Period. No matter what your reasons are and no matter how much sense they make to you, it is NOT okay to be a bully.

Once you've done that, do not say to yourself, "I'm a bully." Say, "I've made a lot of mistakes, but I want to change."

Go to God and pour it all out. Ask God to forgive you. Ask him to help you push RMG stuff from yourself so you can be filled with love and compassion and real joy. Do this every day.

Ask an adult you trust to help you figure out why you are mean to people. There could be a lot of reasons. Maybe you are bullied at home. Perhaps you were bullied at your last school, and you aren't going to let it happen again. Could be you're so afraid people are going to find out something weak in you, you try to show them how powerful you are. You might even think people in general are out to hurt you, so you might as well hurt them first. Whatever your reasons, you probably won't be able to sort them out yourself. Please find a grown-up who will help you, not tell you you'd just better shape up.

While you're working on yourself with a helper, do these things as you are strong enough:

* Go to the girls you've hurt and ask for their forgiveness. Don't expect them all to hug you and say, "Oh, it's okay." What matters is that you do it. It will soften you inside.

* Tell your bully-mates that you aren't going to be mean to other girls anymore. If that means they don't want to be your friends now, that's okay. They weren't your true buds to begin with. You might be alone for a while, but as people see that you're really working on your meanness issues, you'll be surprised who will want to be around you. After all, you have a lot of personal power, and people like that when it's used the Jesus way.

* Get rid of anything in your life that triggers mean behavior on your part. If you swear, make a vow to stop cussing. If you get mad when you play sports, back off on playing until you have more control. If certain people just bring out the worst in you, avoid them. It's hard, but it's going to be worth it when you can do all the things you enjoy, and let other people enjoy them too.

* Keep a mirror in your pocket or backpack. Every time you feel that strong urge to tell someone just exactly what you

think is wrong with her, pull out your mirror and sneer into it.

"It's easy to see a smudge on your neighbor's face and be oblivious to the ugly sneer on your own. Do you have the nerve to say, 'Let me wash your face for you,' when your own face is distorted by contempt? Wipe that ugly sneer off your own face, and you might be fit to offer a washcloth to your neighbor."

– Matthew 7:3–5 (*The Message*)

Those are hard words to hear, but they encourage you to only allow yourself to poke a finger at somebody else's faults when you don't have any of your own. And when is THAT gonna happen? When you do need to talk to a friend about her friendship flubs, the mirror will help you not to do it

It's actually possible to be a Christian bully. Seriously. If you look down on girls who don't know Christ, harshly excluding them from your circle of church friends, telling them God doesn't love them, or gossiping that they're atheists, honey, you are NOT following Christ. He threw a huge fit right in the temple because religious cliques were doing those very things. Pray for girls who haven't gotten to know God yet. Be willing to talk to them about how great God is if they want to hear. Even invite them to church. But if you act as if they are poison ivy, that's bullying. Stop.

with a sneer on your face, that "lovely" expression you see in your reflection.

You're Good to Go

Time to figure out if you and your BFFs are, as a group, bullies, bullied, or bystanders. Get the crew together and do the following:

What you'll need:

+ this book
+ paper and pens for everyone or one big piece of paper and markers
+ honesty
+ brave hearts

What to do:

Do the "That Is SO Me" survey as a group (on pages 91–92). Try to come to an agreement on each item. Your answers may be different from what you starred on your own.

If as a group you are bystanders—you see bullying happening to other people but you haven't done anything to stop it—write down the names of the RMGs who you have observed. Do not gossip about them. Once you've established who they are, let it go for now. At this point, you're ready for the next chapter.

If as a group you discover you are bullies, use the steps in this chapter under "Here's the Deal If You Are a Bully" to write out a five-step plan for shaking the bully habit. Make the steps things you can actually check off as you complete them (not just "don't bully anymore").

If as a group you find that you are the bullied, use the steps in this chapter under "Here's the Deal If You Are a Bully" to write out a five-step plan for becoming bully-free. Make the steps things you can actually check off as you complete them (not just "don't let it bother us anymore").

What it tells you:

✧ Maybe what you do on your own is different from what you do as a group, which can be either a good thing or a not-so-good thing.

✧ You are not alone as you try to make changes.

✧ Once you start being honest with each other, being your best selves becomes easier, and being your not-so-best selves gets harder!

What to do now:

Bystanders — go on to the next chapter, which is especially important for you. Try to read it as a group.

Bullies — as a group or pair, take your five steps, which could involve some time. Go ahead and read the next chapter, because it will give you even more reasons to make progress. But focus for now on really accomplishing your five-step plan.

Bullied — as a group or pair, take your five steps, which won't happen overnight. Go ahead and read the next chapter, because it will encourage you. But focus for now on completing your five-step plan.

Everyone — ask an adult you all trust to be your mentor in this. She won't take the steps for you, but she'll be there to support you and keep you going. After all, she's probably been where you are.

That's What I'm Talkin' About!

Write about what happens after you start on your plan.

I feel a lot more (or less) _____

_____

_____

_____

One thing that has changed is _____

_____

_____

_____

We have gotten help from _____

_____

_____

_____

_____

chapter six

There Are No
INNOCENT BYSTANDERS!

Emily slid down the wall outside her classroom until she was sitting on the floor. That was her place to hang out before school now. Most of the "cool" people stood around by the big plant down the hall, which meant Emily was safe from the Price Tag Girls.

She pulled a chapter book out of her backpack and tried to read it, but as usual lately she couldn't really concentrate. Besides, the girls in the story were best friends, and Emily had a hard time even thinking about that without feeling like she was going to cry.

"You okay?" someone said above her.

Emily blinked away tears and looked up. It was Tia, the new girl. She pointed to the floor beside Emily.

"Can I sit with you?" she said.

Taking a stiff breath, Emily said, "Only if you aren't going to tell me what everybody is saying about me. I already know, believe me."

Tia gave an uncomfortable-sounding cough and sank down next to Emily.

"That's what I wanted to talk to you about," she said. "I don't think what they're saying is true."

Emily couldn't help letting her eyes bulge, but she didn't say anything. Maybe this was a setup.

"Katy and those girls are not nice," Tia said. "I've heard them planning their attacks on you. Did you know they, like, pumped Lara for information so they could spread it around and say that YOU told those secrets about her?"

"I sort of figured that," Emily said.

"They're so evil. Personally, I think they're just using Lara to get to you."

"I don't know what I ever did to them!" Emily said. And then she bit her lip. Could she really trust Tia? So far, everybody else, including Mary Elizabeth and Kimberly, had turned against her.

Tia pulled a breakfast bar out of the pocket of her hoodie. "Want half?"

Emily shook her head. Tia unwrapped it thoughtfully.

"Of course, I don't know because I'm new, but it seems like Katy is jealous of you."

"Of me?" Emily laughed for the first time in days, although it wasn't a feel-good laugh.

"You're cute and you get A's and you're good at sports." Tia shrugged. "She has to practically force people to be her friends, but you had a best friend — "

"That's right — *had*."

"So Katy stole her from you and then made it so no one else would be friends with you either." Tia licked her fingers and then went on. "I knew a girl like that in my old school. She was evil too."

"*Lara* isn't evil," Emily said.

"Whatever. By the way, here they come."

Emily didn't look up, but she could hear the chorus of flip-flops that signaled the P.T.s were near.

"I'm gonna go," Emily said. She started to get up, but Tia put her hand on her arm.

"Don't let them run you off. They won't bother you if I'm here. They don't hate me yet."

Katy's voice rose just a few yards from where they sat. "Would you quit following me everywhere!"

I was here first, Emily thought. But when Katy didn't step toward her, Emily looked at her through her bangs. Katy wasn't talking to her. She was speaking to Lara.

"It's like every place I go, there you are. I can hardly breathe."

Emily stared. Lara kept her eyes on her painted toenails and drew her shoulders up around her ears.

"I thought we were friends," Lara said in a voice Emily could barely hear.

"We were. *Were*," Katy said.

"Past tense," one of the other Tags said. "Get it?"

As far as Emily could see, Lara didn't "get it," because she looked at Katy with pleading eyes. Emily had never seen her look so hurt. Ever.

"I don't understand!" Lara said. "What did I do?"

Katy put her hands over her ears. "She's whining," she said. "Make it stop!"

"If I were you," a Price Tag Girl said to Lara, "I'd shut up."

"Yeah, really," somebody else chimed in.

Each of them took a step toward Lara, except Katy herself, who stayed back and looked as if she'd just snagged the last cookie. Emily's stomach churned. Lara seemed so small and defenseless.

"We're out of here," Katy said. She pointed to Lara. "All but you. Stay away from us or you are SO gonna regret it."

Katy did some weird twist of her hand above her head, and the P.T.s followed her back down the hall. If Lara knew Emily was behind her, she didn't show it. She just slapped her hand over her mouth and tore past. Emily watched the restroom door slap closed behind her, but not before she heard Lara start to cry. She'd know that sound anywhere — just like she knew everything else about her.

"Well," Tia said. "That was interesting."

"It was horrible!" Emily started again to scramble to her feet.

"You're not going after her, are you?" Tia said.

"Hello-o! You saw what they just did to her. I know how that feels!"

Tia yanked at Emily's jeans until she sat back down. "Think about it," she said. "Doesn't she kind of deserve it, after what she did to you?"

"I don't know. They were just so mean."

"And they're always going to be mean because that's just the way they are." Tia put her face close to Emily's. "If you start helping Lara, that's only gonna make it worse for you. You might think they've hurt you as much as they can, but you haven't seen anything yet." Tia shrugged again. "At least that's what I think."

"I don't know what to do," Emily said.

"Don't do anything. It's not your problem." She held up the half-eaten bar. "You sure you don't want the other half of this?"

Emily shook her head. She might never eat again.

GOT GOD?

Tia is content to be a bystander when it comes to bullying. Emily doesn't know *what* to do. But if somebody doesn't do *something*, Katy and her Price Tag Girls are going to go on putting down and tearing up girls whenever they want to. Who knows, Tia herself could be next.

God is very clear that you need to take action when a girl is being mistreated by RMGs:

"This is war, and there is no neutral ground.... If you're not helping, you're making things worse."

—Matthew 12:30 (*The Message*)

Wait! Don't gather every girl you know and arm yourselves to go after the RMGs! Jesus isn't saying you should declare war on the bullies. He's telling you to fight against bullying itself.

Don't let evil get the best of you; get the best of evil by doing good.

—Romans 12:21 (*The Message*)

Get the best of evil, not the evil *person*. And make that happen by *doing good*.

Before you read on to find out what that can look like in your situation, be sure your mind is ready.

Whatever is true, whatever is noble, whatever is right, whatever is pure, whatever is lovely, whatever is admirable – if anything is excellent or praiseworthy – think about such things.... Put [them] into practice. And the God of peace will be with you.

—Philippians 4:8-9

That gives new meaning to the word *whatever*, doesn't it? Fill your head, your heart, yourself with good stuff—God stuff—and you won't go charging in like, well, like a bully. Helping girls who are being bullied is all about taking away the power of bullying. That's true and noble and right and pure and admirable. It's excellent, and God will help you. If you fill yourself with thoughts of getting revenge, seeing RMGs go down, and taking over their turf, don't count on God to back you up.

... For Standing Up against Bullying

There have always been RMGs and peer abuse, but that doesn't mean it's okay. There used to be slavery in the US, but somebody put a stop to it, right? Yours can be the generation that stops *this* cruel behavior, so that you and the girls who come after you can grow up without being scarred by your own kind! Here's how:

Refuse to participate in any kind of bullying yourself. You probably wouldn't intentionally try to hurt someone, but it's possible to become part of the very thing you're so against. Be careful about these negative habits.

Don't put labels on people when you talk about them (popular kids, girly girls, wannabes, freaks, losers). Labels belong on tennis shoes, not people. Look at everyone as an individual. It's even important to be careful when thinking of a really mean girl as a "bully." You have to know that she is a girl who bullies, but don't forget that she probably has her good qualities too.

Make it clear that you will not repeat a rumor. Walk away when girls start gossiping. Better yet, announce that you won't even listen to it. If you're there, you're part of it. If you're not, who are they gonna gossip to?

Don't laugh at put-down jokes, even if the person being dissed isn't there to hear.

Get to know kids in your class and school who aren't part of your group and encourage your friends to do the same. It will make you less likely to allow other people to be mean to them. Your school atmosphere will become more like that of a family than a competitive battleground.

Be careful who you follow as a leader. In fact, when it comes to friends, be your own leader. Don't let anyone else control how you treat people.

Always tell other people that you think bullying is wrong — in a loud voice if you have to. Don't attack the bully, just the bullying.

Ask other people to stop standing by and doing nothing when they see bullying. There's no need to be afraid you'll ALL become the next target, because soon there will be more of you than there are of the bullies.

Include people who seem friendless. They are prime targets for bullies, and you can stop it before it starts by helping an isolated girl build her confidence. In fact, make it your mission never to let anyone feel left out. That's what Jesus did. That kind of generous living spreads, and other girls will start doing it too. Keep thinking about what Jesus said.

Remember that if a girl ignores her bully, the bully will find someone else to be mean to. Your attitude about bullying can give the bully no place to go where her bad treatment will be tolerated.

Get yourself an anti-bullying buddy (or group) and decide that as a team you will take action when you see bullying. You can't change this ugly pattern by yourself. There are always more "girls in the middle" than there are either bullies or victims. You have numbers on your side, so get organized!

> "Whenever you did one of these things to someone overlooked or ignored, that was me — you did it to me."
>
> — Matthew 25:40 (*The Message*)

Now you're ready to help another girl stand up to bullies. Here are some ways you can take action:

Apologize to the girl who's been harmed in the past if you were there and you did nothing to stop it. Assure her that you won't let the bullying continue.

Rather than get all feisty for a fight, be as genuinely nice, friendly, and inclusive to the girl as you can, even if she does annoying things or you and your friends have nothing in common with her. You don't have to be her BFF. Just let her know she's safe from ugly talk and physical harm when she's with you. Sometimes the bullying will stop once the RMG sees that her target has friends.

If your bullied friend is afraid to go someplace in school because she knows the RMGs will abuse her with their words and mean looks, go with her as a group. Surround her with laughter and happy chatter. Just by being with her, you'll make it impossible for a bully and her buddies to get to her. No need to make a verbal statement, like, "Just so you know, your bullying days are over." Shield the bullied girl with your love. That's all.

If the bully does her thing right there in front of you, THEN stand up to her. Be calm. Be polite. Get your friends to back you up. Look her straight in the eye, but don't do anything threatening. Simply say, "Look, this is wrong, and we're not going to stand by and let you control people anymore. You're SO better than that. We just don't have to have bullying in our school."

Your next step is to help the bullied girl stand up for herself the next time, especially when she doesn't have you with her. Take her through chapter 5. Do role plays with her so she feels what it's like to be assertive. If she knows you have her back, she'll have more confidence. Love does that for people.

Meanwhile, encourage the bullied girl to talk to an adult at the place where it's happening (school, church, sports team, etc.). It's important to make the grown-ups in charge aware of what's going on, even if you don't want them to intervene yet. If they don't take her seriously, feel free to show them this book. Tell them that you want to stamp out bullying totally, not just get a particular bully in trouble. You're bound to find support. What adult doesn't want a bully-free environment for kids?

If you have other girls working with you against bullying in general, especially if you've involved adults, there is no need to be afraid that if you help a victim, you'll be the bully's next target. With so much energy working against her plan, she's not going to chance taking it out on you. If she tries to do it in secret, such as on the Internet, you'll all know it's her anyway. She can't hurt you. Her power is false. If she does manage to get a dig in, remember this: "If with heart and soul you're doing good, do you think you can be stopped? Even if you suffer for it, you're still better off" (1 Peter 3:13, The Message).

If things turn really ugly—somebody starts hitting or a mob forms—get an adult IMMEDIATELY. It doesn't matter if it's the maintenance guy, some mom passing through, or the principal's secretary, get the nearest grown-up. That is not something kids should try to handle on their own.

You now know how to deal with a bully, so proceed with courage! Don't wait for adults to come up with a way to stop bullying. You have authority too. Take responsibility.

If you and your friends really want to make wiping out bullying your mission (and you're doing it to help people, not just to form your own powerful clique), write a pledge that anyone can take who wants to join you. And ask your principal if you can post it in your school. The way to make this the most effective is to have people sign it and display it with the signatures. Anyone looking at that will know she doesn't have a chance to get away with bullying!

Here's an example of what that pledge might look like:

As part of my community and my school, I will

✓ pledge to be part of the solution;

✓ eliminate taunting from my own behavior;

✓ encourage others to do the same;

✓ be more sensitive to other people's feelings;

✓ set an example of a caring individual;

✓ not let my words or actions hurt other people; and

✓ stand up for those who are being mistreated.

Signed: _____

You are not forming an alliance AGAINST anyone. You are forming one FOR a world that is safe and accepting—where people can be who they are. You can be part of the generation that stops the hate.

That Is SO Me

Put a star (*) beside each action you think you could take. You probably won't star all of them because different people are good at different things. Don't be afraid to imagine yourself a little out of your comfort zone, though.

I think I could

_____ say hi to a girl other people are mean to.

_____ invite a girl who gets picked on in the cafeteria to sit with me at lunch.

_____ tell a bully she has no right to keep a girl from having peace at school.

_____ start a group whose mission is to stop the bullying.

_____ join an anti-bullying group.

_____ sign an anti-bullying pledge.

_____ make a pledge with my best friend or group of friends not to gossip, spread rumors, use labels, or laugh at put-down jokes.

_____ walk with a girl so she can go where she needs to in school.

_____ be part of a group that shields a girl from bullies who block her path.

_____ encourage a bullied girl to talk to a trusted adult or even go with her.

_____ use my blog or online journal to spread good news instead of bad.

_____ use my blog or online journal to speak out against bullying without mentioning any names.

_____ apologize to a bullied girl I didn't help when she needed it.

_____ pray for the bullies and the bullied alike, as well as for courage for me to stand up for what's right.

Choose one of the things you starred and just do it. Start small. Then do something bigger. Don't try to do it all at once. Do what you can, and you'll be able to do more. Every step you take will make a difference.

You're Good to Go

There isn't room in this book for all the things Jesus said about how people should treat each other. There's so much more good stuff that will really help you with friend and bully issues. Why not find some for yourselves?

What you'll need:

✧ a Bible for each person (the girls can bring their own if they have them)
✧ paper and a pen for each person (go for fun colors if you want)
✧ snacks (just because food brings people together!)

What to do:

Turn to what is known as the Sermon on the Mount, Matthew 5:1–7:27. Divide the reading up into sections, or have one of you read and the others write things down.

Find at least five things Jesus says to do that will make you a good friend—not only to people you like, but to the world. Try to find ideas not mentioned in this book and write them in your own words.

Example: "Let your light shine before men, that they may see your good deeds and praise your Father in heaven" (Matthew 5:16). Shine by doing good things for people so they'll know, you've got God! Girls for God make great friends.

HINT: In Matthew 5:3 – 12, Jesus is not giving instructions, but he is saying that he understands how tough it is just being a person. He's assuring you that no matter how hard things get, God will help you, and you'll come out even better in the end. Read that part, but start your search with verse 13.

What it tells you:

This activity will teach you that it is not just *nice* if you treat people well, it's *required* of a follower of Christ! But it also shows you exactly HOW to do it, and ya gotta love that.

What to do now:

Choose one of your five instructions from Jesus and, with your friends, focus on that for a week. If you pick "shining like lights by doing good deeds," plan what good deeds you'll do, or come up with a signal you'll use when one of you sees an opportunity. Remember not to do this like a competition to see who can outdo who in being super-Christian! Do it because, well, that's what you do.

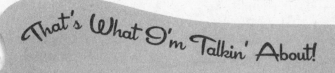

That's What I'm Talkin' About!

In the days ahead, write, draw, or doodle your responses to what happens with your friends.

My favorite thing I did was _____

_____

_____

_____

_____

I know it made a difference (or didn't make a difference) because _____

_____

_____

_____

My friends and I feel _____

_____

_____

_____

_____

chapter seven

From Now On ...

From her desk, Emily watched the classroom door, but even after the bell rang, Lara didn't come in. When Mrs. Jackson came to her name on the roll, she looked around and said, "Has anybody seen Lara?"

Katy and the Price Tag Girls smirked at each other. Tia became very busy with her shoelace, although Emily was sure it hadn't been untied. Mary Elizabeth and Kimberly just looked at the teacher with blank faces.

Mrs. Jackson waited, eyebrows raised. Slowly, Emily raised her hand. "I saw her go into the girls' bathroom."

"Would you go find her, please?" Mrs. Jackson said, and she marched impatiently to her desk for the hall pass. "Honestly, you girls and your drama."

It occurred to Emily as she hurried down the hall that Mrs. Jackson must have known stuff was going on among the girls in the class. *Why hadn't she done something about it?*

Emily stopped with her hand on the door. She wasn't sure what *she* was going to do about it. She had to bring Lara back to the room, but beyond that, she had no idea.

At first she didn't think Lara was there, and then she found her sitting on the floor in the corner by the sinks, curled up in a ball. Her eyes were so puffy from crying they were nearly swollen shut. Emily hadn't seen her look like that since her dog, Lucky, died. She didn't move when Emily squatted in front of her.

"Mrs. Jackson wants you to come to class," she said.

"I can't," Lara said, words coming out in hiccups.

Emily couldn't blame her. She wouldn't want to go anywhere in this condition either.

"What do you want me to tell her?" It struck Emily that this was the first conversation she'd had with Lara in a whole week. She felt like a robot.

"I don't care," Lara said.

Emily felt a pain in her chest. She wasn't sure whether it was from feeling sorry for Lara or from being angry that she would be so upset over those Price Tags.

"I didn't know you cared that much about Katy and them," Emily said stiffly.

Lara shook her head. Tears spilled off the sides of her face. "That's not why I'm crying."

"Oh."

"I'm crying because I did so many mean things to you, and I want to be your friend again, but now you probably hate me."

Emily swallowed hard. All the possible things she could say tumbled through her head.

"I don't hate you." "Is this just because they dumped you?" "Maybe I don't like you so much anymore." "Maybe I should make you suffer the way you did me." "I love you, Lara. Let's just forget the whole thing!"

Emily didn't know which voice to listen to, so she just said, "Why *did* you do it? I don't get it."

Lara leaned her head back against the wall and closed her eyes, although it was hard to tell since they were already in slits.

"That day on the bus, Katy just started talking to me ... and she really did seem nice ... I thought maybe we were wrong about her."

Right, Emily thought. But she just nodded.

"And then you got all jealous, and that made me feel like I couldn't even talk to somebody else."

Emily didn't argue with her. It was kind of true.

"So when she invited me to be in her social studies group, I said yes. I thought I could bring you too, and you would see that it was okay for us to have other friends. Only Katy said no, and, I don't know, I was just afraid to say anything."

Emily knew what she meant. She sat beside Lara and said, "Go on."

"Well, then it was like you and Mary Elizabeth and Kimberly were all mad at me, and Katy and them said you guys weren't treating me right."

Emily grunted. *Like the P.T.s would know anything about that.*

"I know it was stupid, but I told them about how you want all of us together all the time, and how sometimes you're, like, the boss of us. And then I told about that one time when your little brother shoved your math homework down the garbage disposal and you threw a sponge at him. Only I said it was a bottle of ketchup — "

"Lara!"

"And that you went after him with the broom."

"I did not!"

"I know. But they were so interested, and I felt like I was cool to them." Lara started to cry again. "I've never been cool, Emily."

"You've *always* been cool, Lara — ever since you were seven years old! Maybe even before that!"

"But you know everybody thinks the Price Tags are the cool group, and I was part of it — at least I thought I was." Lara sat up straight. "You know what? I think they just used me. They told me people were saying you and I would, like, have nervous breakdowns if we were separated. Now I think they just said that so I'd tell them all this stuff that made me different from you, like that your real name is Emily Ellen and I thought it was a baby name — which I don't. And then they twisted it all around — "

"Yeah," Emily said, "I know."

Lara's voice seemed to come from someplace down inside her. "I'm so sorry, Em. I really am. I know you hate me, but will you please forgive me?"

She was crying so hard, it scared Emily. She got up, grabbed some paper towels, and soaked them in cold water. She handed them to Lara to put on her face, but Lara just squeezed them and looked into Emily's eyes with forty times more pleading than she'd had for Katy.

"What I really want is for us to be friends again," she said. "Could we please, please do that?"

Emily looked at the floor until the tiles all ran together before her eyes. What in the world should she do?

now what?

Let's leave Emily there while we look one last time at Girl Politics. After you've read this chapter, you'll have a chance to help her, in "That's What I'm Talkin' About."

GOT GOD?

You've read a lot of Scripture in this book, and you've even discovered some for yourself. Your mind is probably like a racetrack with all those verses tearing around in there. Jesus knew it was hard to keep it all straight, which is why he gave us a summary of the Law. He boiled it all down to just a few things we absolutely have to do in order to be the kind of friends God wants us to be.

If at any time you face a Girl Politics problem, and you can't remember the suggestions for it in this book, just do this: Love with everything you have. That's what God does. That's what Jesus showed us to do. He said to think about how you want other people to treat you, and treat them that way.

> "'Love the Lord your God with all your heart and with all your soul and with all your mind and with all your strength.' The second is this: 'Love your neighbor as yourself.' There is no commandment greater than these."
>
> – Mark 12:30-31

If a friend is careless with your feelings, love her enough to tell her how you feel. Wouldn't you want her to tell you if it were the other way around?

If a girl looks lonely, love her enough to ask her how she's doing. Wouldn't you want somebody to do that to you if you were alone?

If somebody bullies you, love her enough not to spit right back in her face. Wouldn't you want somebody to control herself if you had a bully moment?

If you see somebody having a hard time with a Really Mean Girl, love her enough to stand up for her. Wouldn't you be just so grateful if someone saved you from humiliation?

> You can't go wrong when you love others. When you add up everything in the law code, the sum total is love.
>
> – Romans 13:10 (*The Message*)

If bullying becomes a problem at your school, love your generation enough to do what you can to stop it. Don't you want somebody to make your school a safe place to be?

Here's the Deal

One more thing. Before you go on to loving everyone from your BFF to the local RMG, don't forget that there are three parts in the summary of the Law:

* Love God
* Love your neighbor
* Love *yourself*

Let's take an important look at that third one. The commandment says to love your neighbor the same way you love yourself.

If the way you treat *yourself* is to put yourself down, force yourself to do things you don't really want to do, or let yourself be ridiculed and not do anything to stop it, then possibly without even realizing it, you might very well treat your neighbor the same way.

If loving yourself is an idea you just can't get your mind around, try reading *Everybody Tells Me to Be Myself but I Don't Know Who I Am,* another Faithgirlz! book. For now, just make sure you realize that loving yourself doesn't mean always putting yourself first, always trying to get your own way, or telling everyone how fabulous you are all the time. It simply means taking good care of the beautiful true self God gave you.

Your true self comes through when these things happen:

* You do the things you really love to do, whether anyone else loves to do them or not.

✳ You are completely at ease, not worrying about how you look or what you're going to say.
✳ You are totally honest.
✳ You hurt, either for yourself or for someone else.
✳ You do something unselfish for someone.
✳ You pray without "performing" for God.

A feeling of joy bubbles up inside you.
You truly like who you are at that moment.
That's the You that you need to love so you can then shine love on everyone else. Here's what that looks like:

❀ You make your own decisions about who you're going to be friends with.
❀ You choose friends who like you just as you truly are, who you never have to "perform" for, even if that means you only have one close friend.
❀ You don't let anyone pressure you into doing or saying anything you know isn't right.
❀ You give up something of your own if someone else truly needs it, including your place in the spotlight.

At the same time, when you love your neighbor as yourself, you never give up who you really are, because no one else ever really needs for you to do that. This is what it might look like when you love your neighbor as yourself without giving up who you are:

❀ Your BFF didn't get her homework done and she asks if she can copy yours. You say no, but that you'll help her do her own before it's time to turn it in.
❀ Your group of friends wants to send a prank email, and you're the only one with her own computer in her room. You say you will absolutely not participate in that, and you don't think they should either.

✿ A friend begs you not to tell anyone that her stepfather is hitting her hard enough to leave bruises. You say she needs help from a grown-up, and you will go with her to get it — or you will tell an adult yourself.

Sometimes loving your neighbor (friend) means saying no to her. You can only know when to do that if you love the real you. Then you can use this question as a guide as you're making friend decisions: *Does this show love for God, the other person, AND my true, honest self?* If the answer is yes, go for it! If the answer is no, go back to the things you've learned in this book. And most important of all, when you make a mistake — and you will because you are a human being — ask God, your neighbor, and yourself for forgiveness. Then keep on growing into the best friend you can possibly be.

That Is SO Me

Here is a list of the main things you've read about in this book. Put a star (*) next to any that you would like to work on in your Friend World.

_____ Having Sister Chicks instead of a Closed Clique (chapter 2).

_____ Handling Friendship Flubs in my group of buds (chapter 3).

_____ Making new friends (chapter 4).

_____ Dealing with people who bully me OR changing my bullying behavior (chapter 5).

_____ Putting a stop to bullying, period (chapter 6).

_____ Being a good friend to myself (chapter 7).

If you have only one star, put a number 1 next to it. If you starred more than one thing, number those items, with 1 being the most important to you and 2 the next most important, 3 the next, and so on.

You may have been working on those things already, especially in the "You're Good to Go" exercises. Don't feel like you have to go after everything at once. Try the activity you put a number 1 by and work on these one by one instead. By the way, if you had no stars, be available to other girls who are working on things, but remember that you are human. There are always ways to be better.

One more "one more thing": Enjoy this work of being in a relationship. For all their griping, the psalm writers did.

These God-chosen lives all around – what splendid friends they make!

– Psalm 16:3 (*The Message*)

Go now, and love those splendid friends!

You're Good to Go

You've worked hard in this book. Now it's time to simply celebrate. Get together with your BFF or group of friends or could-be friends. Think about inviting a girl or two who doesn't have buds, even if you have plenty.

Before you meet, ask each girl to bring something that shows how much she loves her friends (or you, if there are just two of you). It can be a food treat, a special card, a banner, something of her own she wants to give away, favors she's made, a song, or maybe a Bible verse for each person. Tell your buds they can be creative. Anything goes, as long as it's loving.

What you'll need:

- everyone's contributions
- celebration decorations if you want them (balloons, shiny streamers, a display of your friends' pictures, whatever)
- time to savor the joy of friendship

What to do:

- ❋ Give each person a chance to share what she's brought.
- ❋ Take your time appreciating each thing.
- ❋ Talk, giggle, hug — maybe even cry happy tears.
- ❋ Simply treasure the love in the room.

What it tells you:

- ☆ How much you have to be thankful for.
- ☆ How important friends are.
- ☆ How even more important it is that you take care of each other.
- ☆ And not just each other, but girls who aren't as blessed as you are right now.
- ☆ That no matter what flubs and other issues you may have to work on, you are a pretty spectacular friend already.

What to do now:

Do exactly what Jesus told us:

"Love one another the way I loved you. This is the very best way to love."

– John 15:12 (*The Message*)

That's What I'm Talkin' About!

Now go back to the beginning of this chapter, where we left Emily trying to decide about Lara ... and for that matter about Mary Elizabeth and Kimberly and Tia and Katy and the Price Tags. Whew! She has a lot to decide.

Help her out. You've packed in a lot of information and ideas while reading this book, so put them to work for Emily. Use that to figure out a plan for her.

Now write the story ending, just the way you see it — as the fabulous friend you are!

_____

_____

_____

_____

_____

_____

_____

_____

_____

_____

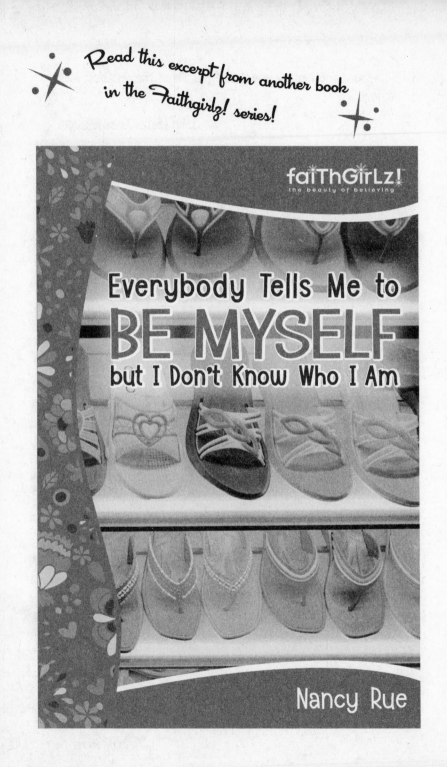

faiThGirLz!
the beauty of believing

Everybody Tells Me to
BE MYSELF
but I Don't Know Who I Am

Nancy Rue

chapter one

Who,
ME?

Molly Ann McPherson trailed her fingers over the contents
of her brand-new suitcase:

A stack of neatly folded — and very cool — shorts.

Another pile of matching tops, the cutest ever.

A pink zipper bag with her own bottles of everything from
shampoo to orange-flavored mouthwash.

And the perfect stationery — shaped like flip-flops — so she
could write home every day.

Her summer dream was packed in that suitcase. But suddenly
Molly shivered in a blast of cold fear.

"I don't think I want to go to camp, Mom," she said.

Molly's mother looked up at her over the swimsuit from
which she was removing the tags. "What?" she said. "All I've
heard from you for the last month is how much camp is going to
rock."

"But I won't know anybody there," Molly said. "What if
everybody thinks I'm a loser? What if I don't make any friends?
What if I get left out of everything?"

Molly's mom shook her head. "Don't be silly, Molly," she said.
"Just be yourself and you'll be fine."

When her mom left to find the sunscreen, Molly stared miserably at the suitcase full of coolness she'd been so excited about.

Be myself? she thought. *Who's Myself?*

Was she the Molly who was careful to do only what the really popular kids did?

Was she the Molly who always agreed with her friends about every little thing?

Was she the girl who secretly dreamed of being a famous lawyer, or the one who took piano lessons because her mom did when she was a kid, or the one who refused to cry in front of anybody, no matter how sad she was?

Molly slumped on her elbows onto her perfect stacks of camp clothes.

"How am I supposed to be myself," she wailed, "when I don't even know who I am?"

now what?

Poor Molly is having a major case of homesickness, and she hasn't even left her house yet. But there's something else going on too, something that can strike any of us, whether we're thousands of miles from our family or sitting in our own bedroom. It's an attack of the "Who Am I's?" and it can be pretty scary.

The good news is that this book is here to help you

* figure out who you really-deep-down-inside are, and

* be that person no matter who you're with.

It's like a vaccine against future attacks.

Right now we have our Molly, suffering the worst case of the "Who Am I's?" ever. If you were there in the room with Molly and her suitcase, what would you say to her? Would you give her advice? Or would you be absolutely clueless what to say because you feel that same way . . . a lot?

Whatever you want to tell Molly, write it in the space below. There are no right or wrong answers, so be honest. If, as you read the rest of this book, you discover something that makes you change your mind about how to encourage Molly, you'll have a chance to "talk" to her again in the very last chapter.

Dear Molly...

Here's the Deal

How many times have *you* heard grown-ups say, "Just be yourself"? Like that's supposed to prepare you for a situation where you don't know anybody, or you don't know what you're supposed to do, or you have that feeling that you are *not* going to fit in at *all*.

In the first place, what do they mean by "be yourself"? They're talking about a thing called *authenticity*. When you're *authentic*,

- ✿ you're completely honest;
- ✿ you don't pretend to be rich, or way smart about something, or totally into horses (or whatever everybody else is into) when you're not;
- ✿ you don't copy the way other kids dress or talk or laugh if it doesn't feel natural to you;
- ✿ you go after the things you're interested in even if nobody else does; and
- ✿ you make up your own mind when it comes to decisions, according to what you know is right and wrong.

That sounds pretty easy, doesn't it? You just do all that stuff and you're authentic.

Yeah, well, if it were that simple, there wouldn't be this book about it, right? Maybe right this very minute you're thinking of one of these problems:

- ✿ What if I'm so honest I hurt people's feelings?
- ✿ What if I just do my thing and everybody thinks I'm weird?
- ✿ What if I always do what's right, and nobody wants to be with me because I'm too "good"?
- ✿ What if I don't even know what I like, and what I'm interested in, and how I want to dress? What about *that*?

Take a big ol' sigh of relief, because this book is here to help you turn every one of those "What Ifs" into a "What Is." You'll learn how to

- ✿ be honest and encouraging at the same time;
- ✿ know what your own "unique thing" is and go for it without caring if other kids think you're weird;
- ✿ show people that "good" is cool; and
- ✿ discover more and more the special, one-of-a-kind person you are... and love you!

Wait... did we just say you're going to love yourself? Isn't that conceited?

Selfish?

Stuck up?

Let's see what God has to say about that.

GOT GOD?

Even if you've only just started thinking about God on your own, you probably know that God-loving people believe God the Creator thought each one of us up, made us, and put us here for a reason. The Bible, where God talks to us, says that over and over. One of the coolest verses is this one:

[God] has shaped each person in turn; now he watches everything we do.
—Psalm 33:15
(The Message)

It's fun to imagine God's magnificent hands making an individual person who is totally different from every other baby girl or boy God has created before. Some like to think of God as a potter, shaping people out of clay. God makes a perfect work of art, breathes life into it, and loves it.

> "Woe to him who quarrels with his Maker... Does the clay say to the potter, 'What are you making?'"
> —ISAIAH 45:9

God loves what God has made: palm trees, snow leopards, mosquitoes (yeah, even those pesky little critters), and you. God loves you, so how can you do any less than love you too?

It's hard, though, with the world telling you to pick yourself apart all the time. Are your clothes hip? Is your slang up-to-date? Are you friendly enough, funny enough, blonde enough? We'll talk more about that later. For now, just remember that God knows how hard it is, which is why God sent Jesus to make everything totally clear. From all the commandments the people had to remember and follow, Jesus got it down to the two most important ones:

> "Love the Lord your God with all your heart and with all your soul and with all your mind." This is the first and greatest commandment. And the second is like it: "Love your neighbor as yourself."
> —MATTHEW 22:37-39

Basically, if you don't love yourself, you're not going to be very good at loving other people. Loving you doesn't mean you're conceited. It's a requirement! In fact, Jesus goes on to say that all the other commandments are based on these two. If you can't love God with everything you have — and love yourself and other people the same way — you don't have a chance of obeying "honor your father and your mother" (Exodus 20:12) or "do not envy" or any of the rest of them. That could get to be a mess.

Here's the way it works in *God's* world:

✦ God made you beautifully unique, right down to your fingerprints, your voice print, and your designer ears.

✦ God gave the Unique You talents and interests.

✦ God shows you who you are as you get to know him better and better. That's the only way to know the Unique You.

IT (Important Thing):
Moses asked God what he wanted the Israelites to call him. What God said translates as, "I AM WHO I AM." That's what he wants you to be too — exactly who you are. He loves that. So should you.

God wants you to figure out what you're here for. It's part of who you are, who God truly made you to be. And it's something you continue to learn all your life—as long as you stick with God.

If you hate who you are and try to be something or someone else, you grow more false. You move further from your true, beautiful self.

When you love somebody, you want to bring that person joy, right? You bring God joy when you let your real personality and talents shine, instead of hiding them and copying somebody else. Any time you reject any part of your real self—maybe the fact that you're naturally quiet or a true leader—you're telling God he didn't know what he was doing when he created you. Hel-lo-o!

Nonfiction

Everybody Tells Me to Be Myself but I Don't Know Who I Am

ISBN 978-0-310-71295-4

This addition to the Faithgirlz! line helps girls face the challenges of being their true selves with fun activities, interactive text, and insightful tips.

Girl Politics

ISBN 978-0-310-71296-1

Parents and kids alike may think that getting teased or arguing with friends is just part of growing up, but where is the line between normal kid stuff and harmful behavior? This book is a guide for girls on how to deal with girl politics, God-style.

The Skin You're In

ISBN 978-0-310-71999-1

Beauty tips and the secret of true inner beauty are revealed in this interactive, inspirational, fun addition to the Faithgirlz! line.

Body Talk

ISBN 978-0-310-71275-6

In a world where bodies are commodities, girls are under more pressure at younger ages. This book is a fun and God-centered way to give girls the facts and self-confidence they need as they mature into young women.

the beauty of believing

Sophie Series
Written by Nancy Rue

Meet Sophie LaCroix, a creative soul who's destined to become a great film director someday. But many times her overactive imagination gets her in trouble!

Check out the other books in the series!

Book 1: Sophie's World
IBSN: 978-0-310-70756-1

Book 2: Sophie's Secret
ISBN: 978-0-310-70757-8

Book 3: Sophie Under Pressure
ISBN: 978-0-310-71840-6

Book 4: Sophie Steps Up
ISBN: 978-0-310-71841-3

Book 5: Sophie's First Dance
ISBN: 978-0-310-70760-8

Book 6: Sophie's Stormy Summer
ISBN: 978-0-310-70761-5

Book 7: Sophie's Friendship Fiasco
ISBN: 978-0-310-71842-0

Book 8: Sophie and the New Girl
ISBN: 978-0-310-71843-7

Book 9: Sophie Flakes Out
ISBN: 978-0-310-71024-0

Book 10: Sophie Loves Jimmy
ISBN: 978-0-310-71025-7

Book 11: Sophie's Drama
ISBN: 978-0-310-71844-4

Book 12: Sophie Gets Real
ISBN: 978-0-310-71845-1

faThGirLz!™
the beauty of believing

A Lucy Novel
Written by Nancy Rue

New from Faithgirlz! By bestselling author Nancy Rue.

Lucy Rooney is a feisty, precocious tomboy who questions everything—even God. It's not hard to see why: a horrible accident killed her mother and blinded her father, turning her life upside down. It will take a strong but gentle housekeeper—who insists on Bible study and homework when all Lucy wants to do is play soccer—to show Lucy that there are many ways to become the woman God intends her to be.

Book 1: Lucy Doesn't Wear Pink
ISBN 978-0-310-71450-7

Book 3: Lucy's Perfect Summer
ISBN 978-0-310-71452-1

Book 2: Lucy Out of Bounds
ISBN 978-0-310-71451-4

Book 4: Lucy Finds Her Way
ISBN 978-0-310-71453-8

Available now at your local bookstore!
Visit www.faithgirlz.com, it's the place for girls ages 9-12.

ZONDERkidz™
.com

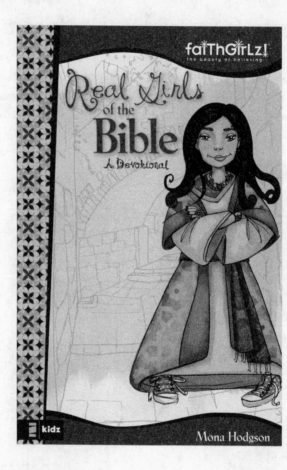

Devotions

No Boys Allowed: Devotions for Girls

Softcover • ISBN 978-0-310-70718-9

This short, ninety-day devotional for girls ages 10 and up is written in an upbeat, lively, funny, and tween-friendly way, incorporating the graphic, fast-moving feel of a teen magazine.

Girlz Rock: Devotions for Girls

Softcover • ISBN 978-0-310-70899-5

In this ninety-day devotional, devotions like "Who Am I?" help pave the spiritual walk of life, and the "Girl Talk" feature poses questions that really bring each message home. No matter how bad things get, you can always count on God.

Chick Chat: Devotions for Girls

Softcover • ISBN 978-0-310-71143-8

This ninety-day devotional brings the Bible right into your world and offers lots to learn and think about.

Shine On, Girl!: Devotions for Girls

Softcover • ISBN 978-0-310-71144-5

This ninety-day devotional will "totally" help teen girls connect with God, as well as learn his will for their lives.

Available now at your local bookstore!
Visit www.faithgirlz.com, it's the place for girls ages 9-12.

Bibles

Every girl wants to know she's totally unique and special. This Bible says that with Faithgirlz! sparkle! Now girls can grow closer to God as they discover the journey of a lifetime, in their language, for their world.

The NIV Faithgirlz! Bible

Hardcover
ISBN 978-0-310-71581-8

Softcover
ISBN 978-0-310-71582-5

The NIV Faithgirlz! Bible

Italian Duo-Tone™
ISBN 978-0-310-71583-2

The NIV Faithgirlz! Backpack Bible

Periwinkle
Italian Duo-Tone™
ISBN 978-0-310-71012-7

Introduce your mom to Nancy Rue!

Today's mom is raising her 8-to-12-year-old daughter in a society that compels her little girl to grow up too fast. *Moms' Ultimate Guide to the Tween Girl World* gives mothers practical advice and spiritual inspiration to guide their mini-women into adolescence as strong, confident, authentic, and God-centered young women; even in a morally challenged society and without losing their childhoods before they're ready.

Nancy Rue has written over 100 books for girls, is the editor of the Faithgirlz Bible, and is a popular speaker and radio guest with her expertise in tween and teen issues. She and husband Jim have raised a daughter of their own and now live in Tennessee.

Visit Nancy at NancyRue.com

Available wherever books are sold.

ZONDERVAN®
.com

We want to hear from you. Please send your comments
about this book to us in care of zreview@zondervan.com. Thank you.

ZONDERVAN.com/
AUTHORTRACKER
follow your favorite authors